ARCHIE KIMPTON

JUMBLE CAT

ILLUSTRATED BY KATE HINDLEY

HOT
KEY
BOOKS

First published in Great Britain in 2014 by Hot Key Books
Northburgh House, 10 Northburgh Street, London EC1V 0AT

A CIP catalogue record for this book is available from the British Library.

ISBN: 978-1-4714-0278-4

1

This book is typeset in 11pt Sabon using Atomik ePublisher
Printed and bound by Clays Ltd, St Ives Plc

FSC

Hot Key Books supports the Forest Stewardship Council (FSC),
the leading international forest certification organisation, and is
committed to printing only on Greenpeace-approved FSC-certified paper.

www.hotkeybooks.com

Hot Key Books is part of the Bonnier Publishing Group
www.bonnierpublishing.com

For Dad, who never lost his voice

Contents

CHAPTER 1

THE SLIPPERS

Do you ever think that something isn't quite right? That the people you live with, your *family*, may not be your family after all? That maybe, just maybe, there was a colossal mix-up in the hospital when you were a baby and you ended up living with a bunch of revolting oddbods who couldn't possibly be related to you?

This is something Billy Slipper thought about every day.

He looked across the breakfast table at his twin sister, Mindy. How on earth could she be his sister? She was practically a different species, let alone his twin. For starters she didn't even look like him, with her blonde hair and a nose so flat and wide it resembled a mushroom clinging to the trunk of a damp tree. Also she was tall, much taller than Billy, and unfortunately much stronger; if ever an argument grew out of hand, she would put him in a headlock and burp loudly into his ear, leaving him half deaf for hours on end.

Billy poured cereal into his bowl and reached for the milk. If Mindy really was his twin sister, then surely they should have some kind of special connection. If Mindy was in pain, would he feel it too? For a moment he thought about kicking her under the table, just to see if it hurt him as well, but something told him that wouldn't be a good idea. As everyone in the Slipper household knew, Mindy's temper was ferocious.

And then it came to him. It was obvious! If she really, really was his twin sister then they should be able to communicate using just the *power of their minds*. Telepathy. He would telepathise her. He put down his spoon and stared hard at Mindy, concentrating, calling her with his mind.

'Mindy,' he telepathised, 'can you hear me?'

Mindy was busy. Her doll, Tina Tippytoes, was not eating her breakfast properly. Every time a tiny piece of cereal fell out of her dolly mouth, Mindy whacked her around the head with a spoon.

Billy tried again. 'Oi! Mindy! Moose face! It's me, Billy!'

But the Slipper Telepathy Line wasn't working.

Eventually Mindy looked up. 'Why are you staring at me? You're such a weirdo.'

'Moose face,' he repeated, but this time he said it out loud.

Predictably, Mindy called for reinforcements. 'Muuuum!' she wailed, grinning wickedly. She knew she was getting her brother into trouble and she loved it. 'Billy called me moose face.'

Ah yes. Mum. Also known as Phillipa Slipper. Also known as Phillipa Slipper Kitty Kicker after her habit of kicking cats that lazed about on the neighbourhood pavements. She hated them. Actually, she hated all animals, but she really had it in for cats.

'Billy!' she barked, shivering with disgust, 'You are not to talk to your sister like that. How you can compare Mindy to a filthy, dirty moose is beyond me. They roll in their own poo, you know.' And she turned back to what she was doing, which was washing carrots, drying them with a hairdryer, then putting each super-clean carrot into its own miniature plastic bag.

Billy said nothing, even when Mindy stuck out her tongue at him. He was used to being told on by his sister and told off by his mother.

That is, if she really was his mother.

Phillipa Slipper was very tall. As tall as any woman Billy had ever seen, and certainly way taller than his dad. She always wore her hair in a bun, coiled tightly on the top of her head, which of course made her look even taller. Like Mindy, her nose was flat and wide, though it looked more like a boxer's squashed nose than a mushroom. But the main thing about Phillipa Slipper was that she *couldn't stand dirt*. Not a speck, a mote nor a microblob of dust escaped her beady eye. If ever a smidgen of filth found its way into her house she dropped to her knees and got scrubbing straight away.

For example, last winter, after a particularly mucky meter reading by the gas man, she insisted on covering her house in plastic sheeting. First she covered the floors, then the skirting boards, then all the walls as high as she could reach.

'At last,' she said as she sat down on the sofa with a cup of tea, 'my house will never be dirty again.'

But that wasn't the end of it. As she sipped her tea she noticed a tiny stain on one of the cushions. It was a microscopic stain, invisible to the normal human eye. But not to Phillipa Slipper. From that moment she started to cover everything in plastic sheeting. The sofa and cushions were first, then the television, the table, chairs, ornaments, even her prized collection of Victorian spatulas, were all covered top to toe in plastic. The kitchen was next, followed by the hallway and the laundry room. Three days later the whole downstairs of the house (apart from the oven and the toaster) was totally swathed in plastic sheeting.

Getting around the house was a noisy business. *Scrunch, scrunch, scrunch* every footstep. Scrunching from the kitchen table to the sink. *Scrunch, scrunch* into the living room. *Scrunch, squeeeeak* as you sat down on the sofa. But Phillipa Slipper wouldn't have it any other way. Her house was immaculate and that was all that mattered.

Billy finished his cereal as fast as possible. When his mother and his sister were around, he spent as little time as possible at home. It was just better that way, and besides, there were far more interesting things to do outside. He put his bowl in the sink and started to make a cheese sandwich for later. Sometimes he spent the whole day wandering in the nearby hills and woods and he didn't want to go hungry.

Picture this. Just as Billy was putting the cheese in between the bread, a solitary crumb rolled off the plate. It fell and landed on the plastic-covered floor, making a sound no louder than an ant fainting on a hot day. Of course Billy hadn't noticed, Mindy hadn't noticed, but . . .

'BILLY!' bellowed Phillipa Slipper.

In an instant, she was on her knees searching for the crumb. Billy stepped back far too quickly and tumbled over her, sending the cheese flying out of his hand. All three watched in horror as it shot up into the air and, SPLAT, stuck to the ceiling, the only place that wasn't covered in plastic sheeting.

This time it was a roar. 'BILLY!'

He scrambled to his feet, grabbed the bread and darted out of the front door, heading for Tumbledown Hill.

CHAPTER 2

TUMBLEDOWN HILL

It was his favourite place. There was nowhere Billy felt happier than in the woods around Tumbledown Hill. He knew it like the back of his hand; each tree and burrow and bird's nest was as familiar to him as his own bedroom, and yet every time he came here, he always discovered something new.

So far, he hadn't had a very successful morning. All that he'd found was a cracked pocket mirror and some bit of old bone that might have belonged to a giant squirrel or possibly a tiny dinosaur. Some days, as he roamed through the woods, he found real treasures. Only last week he'd found a dried-up stag beetle, an enormous acorn, some marbles and a leaf in the shape of Italy, all on the same day. These were the sorts of things he took home. His mother called it useless junk. He called these treasures his 'Collectabillya' and they sprawled all round his bed, along the floor and right up to the edge of the skipping rope that Mindy had stretched across the room, dividing his half of the bedroom from hers. When Mindy was out, he would lie on his bed and daydream about his Collectabillya – dream about hunchbacks playing marbles in the woods, or escaped Italian convicts weeping at the sight of the boot-shaped leaf, or giant stag beetles using Mindy's head as a ping-pong ball.

He trudged out of the woods and crossed a field towards the bottom of Tumbledown Hill. After the cool air of the woods the afternoon sun felt warm on his skin. He lay down in the long grass, closed his eyes and thought about who might win a fight between the giant squirrel and the tiny dinosaur.

Just as the squirrel was getting the upper hand, trapping the dinosaur in an eye-popping headlock, Billy heard something. It was a strange, eerie cry. Certainly not human. He sat up and looked around.

Apart from a dog walker in a faraway field there was nobody about. It must have been the tiny dinosaur squealing in pain, he told himself. It sometimes happened; really good daydreams got muddled up with real life. He lay down in the grass again and went back to the fight. He'd missed a bit. Now the dinosaur had got hold of some stinging nettles and was shovelling them down the squirrel's pants, though why the squirrel was wearing pants was anyone's guess. The fight was hotting up.

There it was again! The same eerie sound, but more urgent this time. He looked up, shielding his eyes from the sun. Near the top of Tumbledown Hill he saw something slipping and sliding down the hill. Billy stood up. It looked like a small animal of some sort, a badger or a hare or maybe . . . a giant squirrel! His very own giant squirrel. He'd take it home and hide it in the shed and feed it giant acorns and dress it in his pants and . . .

Just then, the creature completely lost its footing. It started rolling down the hill, slowly at first, disappearing into thick tussocks of grass, then re-emerging, still tumbling, gathering speed like a runaway train, bumping over hillocks, through brambles, getting faster and faster, coming straight at him. Whatever it was, Billy was determined to catch it. He steadied himself, spreading his arms out wide like a goalkeeper preparing to save a penalty.

THWACK! It crashed into Billy's stomach with enormous force, knocking him to the ground. He was winded, but somehow, whatever it was, he'd caught it. He lay there a while trying to catch his breath, the creature kerplumped across his stomach, as heavy as a sack full of cauliflowers.

Billy counted to thirty and then, without making any sudden movements, slowly lifted his head to take a peek.

It was a cat. Well, he thought it was a cat, but it was like no cat he'd ever seen. Everything was in the wrong place. The head was where a leg should be, the tail was where the head should be and the legs were sticking out all over the place. It was a totally jumbled-up cat.

As if it had been sleeping all along, the cat yawned, opened its eyes and stared directly at Billy.

'What are you looking at?' demanded the cat. Its wide, green eyes were inches from Billy's face.

Billy froze. He stared back at the cat, trying to think of something to say. What *do* you say to a jumbled-up cat that talks?

'Cats can't talk,' stuttered Billy, eventually.

'Of course cats can't talk,' said the cat, talking.

'But you're talking.'

'Am I?' replied the cat. It seemed genuinely surprised.

Billy sat up. The jumbled-up cat slid down Billy's chest and onto his lap.

'I'm hungry,' announced the cat.

Billy felt his pocket. 'I've got a cheese sandwich we can share. But there isn't any cheese in it. It got stuck on the ceiling.'

He couldn't believe he was telling a cat about the cheese. Nonetheless, he took the two slices of bread out of his pocket, gave one to the cat and kept the other for himself. Hungrily, they ate the bread together as if it were the most normal thing in the world.

'Where did you come from?' asked Billy.

'The top of the hill,' said the cat as it licked the crumbs off Billy's trousers.

'No. I mean before that.'

The cat thought for a moment. 'I don't know. But I'm here now.'

Billy studied the cat again, closer this time. It was ginger with patches on each of its paws as if it had walked through a puddle of white paint. Its tail was striped like a tiger and, if the truth be told, it was rather fat. Apart from its slightly crumpled whiskers, the cat didn't seem to be injured by the fall. But the legs, head and tail were clearly all jumbled up. It reminded him of a plastic doll called Dobbie his sister used to have. At bath time, he'd pull off Dobbie's head, arms and legs and put them back in the wrong sockets. He didn't do it *just* to annoy Mindy – the doll looked more interesting, that's all. Annoying Mindy was a bonus.

'Don't you have anything else I can eat?' asked the cat, a little bit rudely. It hadn't even thanked him for the bread yet.

'No, I'm afraid not.'

'Nothing at all? Not even a sweet?'

Billy shook his head.

'What about a cough sweet? You must have a cough sweet?'

'But I don't have a cough,' replied Billy. 'Nor do you.'

Immediately the cat started making the most peculiar rasping noises.

'Kaaarrup! Kaaarrup! Aaairr kaaarrup!'

Billy giggled. He'd heard cats sneezing before, but never one pretending to have a cough.

'It's not funny. I actually have a nasty cough.'

'I'm sorry,' said Billy, still smiling.

'It's probably cat flu and if I die it'll be your fault. One measly cough sweet, that's all I wanted.'

Billy remembered the bone he'd found that morning, the one from the giant squirrel or the tiny dinosaur.

'I've got this,' he said, holding the bone close to the cat's nose.

The cat sniffed and screwed up its nose in disgust. 'Is that it?' It really was very rude.

'If you like, you could come back to my house and get something to eat there,' suggested Billy.

'How thrilling. A delicious feast of bread and old bone in your house,' the cat replied sarcastically. 'No thanks, dog breath, I'm a cat with standards. I'm off.'

And with that the cat tried to clamber off Billy's lap. Its legs flapped around in the air and its tail swished around like a helicopter, but it just couldn't get up.

'You're all jumbled up,' explained Billy. 'I don't think you can walk.'

'Don't be ridiculous. Of course I can walk.'

The cat tried even harder this time, but only managed to tumble off Billy's lap onto the grass.

'What's happened to me?' whimpered the cat as

it tried to stand on all fours. 'Why can't I get up?'

Billy remembered the cracked pocket mirror he'd found that morning. He opened it and held it up to the cat's face.

Now everyone knows that cats can jump very high, especially when they're scared, but nobody, not even the world's greatest cat expert (whose name is Professor Funkleschnit, and he knows everything about cats) could have guessed how high this jumbled-up cat would jump. The instant it looked in the mirror its legs sprang out in all directions. Two of the legs pushed off against the ground, sending it spinning up into the sky, higher than Billy, twice the height of Billy.

'MEEEARRRGHH!'

It landed with a thud in the tall grass.

'What's happened to me?' wailed the cat for the second time. Its fur was all puffed up as if it had been sticking its tongue into an electricity socket. It turned and glared at Billy. 'This is all your fault. I was fine until you came along with your empty sandwiches and your cheesy promises. Well don't just stand there, you fat-faced flop. Do something!'

As best he could, Billy wrapped his cardigan around the furious, frightened, foul-mouthed animal, picked it up and set off for home.

CHAPTER 3

A NEW PADDLING POOL

Every morning at three thirty, Christopher Slipper climbed into his milk float and set off for work. From his bed, Billy listened to his dad leaving. He liked hearing the sound of the electric vehicle whirring away down the road and the empty milk bottles clinking together in their crates. When Christopher Slipper got home from his milk round, he poured himself a large glass of milk, sat down on the sofa and watched quiz shows on television until seven o'clock. Then he went to bed. And that was it. Every day the same. He used to spend his weekends tinkering away in the shed, but ever since Phillipa Slipper complained about the 'dust and filth' he brought back into the house, he gave that up and spent the whole weekend silently watching TV.

By the time Billy got home it was nearly seven o'clock. His arms ached; the cat was heavy and awkward to carry, what with its legs sticking out each and every way. On top of that, it didn't stop asking questions all the way home – 'Are we there yet?' or 'When's dinner?' or 'Are we there yet?' again and again. Billy crept round the side of the house and peered in through the window, just in time to see his dad get up from the sofa, turn off the television and leave the room. Billy counted to twenty, went round to the front and quietly opened the door.

It was Tuesday, so he knew his mother would be out. She had enrolled on a course, 'Pest Control for Beginners', that ran every Tuesday in the town hall. Each week she came home with new and efficient ways to eliminate pests from her house. For instance, in week three she discovered that stink bugs can live in men's beards for months on end. So that very evening, as soon as she got home, she woke up Christopher Slipper, sent him to the bathroom and ordered him to shave off his beard there and then. No arguments. Every last bit of bug-infested stubble fuzz. When he finished, she sent him back to bed and set to work. She swept the floor and scrubbed the sink and just to make sure, she poured a whole bottle of bleach down the plughole.

'We don't want any stink bugs living in the pipes. Urgh! The thought of it!'

Just another day in the Slipper household.

With the cat under his arm, Billy scrunched his way up the hallway. At the bottom of the stairs he stopped and listened. He could hear Mindy jabbering in the bedroom, which probably meant she was putting her dolls to bed. She went through the same routine every evening; good dolls slept on the shelf above her bed, but if a doll had been naughty during the day, heaven forbid. The naughty doll's arm or leg was given three sharp twists in the pencil sharpener followed by a night in the isolation shoebox under her bed, thereby allowing the wicked doll plenty of time to think about its behaviour. Some of her naughtier dolls, Lady Crimplene Posh, for instance, no longer had arms and legs, but four useless pointy stumps.

In the kitchen, Billy put the cat on a chair and opened the fridge. The Slipper fridge had to be the tidiest fridge in the world. Everything was perfectly arranged. All the jars and bottles were kept in straight lines, the yoghurts in neat little piles and each individual vegetable was wrapped in its own bag. In a labelled Tupperware box on the bottom shelf, Billy found six cooked chicken drumsticks. He gave one to the cat and sat down beside it.

As they ate, Billy thought about what to do next.

He couldn't hide the animal from his sister in their shared bedroom; Mindy would be sure to find it and scream the house down. He could try the attic, but if the cat moved about too much then his mother would assume they had rats and have the whole attic fumigated.

'More chicken,' demanded the cat.

The garden shed was a possibility, or maybe . . .

'That's it!' he cried. 'Mrs Mandiddee!'

'Mrs Whodiddee?' queried the cat.

'Mrs Mandiddee. She lives next door. You can stay with her for a few days until we work out what to do with you.'

'Why can't I stay here?' asked the cat. There was a gloopy piece of chicken stuck to the side of its mouth. 'Does Mrs Mandiddee have chicken? I want chicken.'

Billy tried to imagine what his mother would do if she ever found this cat in her house. Eating her chicken too. The idea was so ridiculous and terrifying he didn't know whether to laugh or cry.

'Come on. Eat up, we should go. My mother will be home soon.'

Just then the front door opened.

Phillipa Slipper was home.

Quick as a shot, Billy grabbed a tea towel and draped it over the cat. Footsteps scrunched along the hallway.

'Don't say a word,' he whispered to the cat. 'Not a squeak.'

Phillipa Slipper stood in the doorway. 'Who are you talking to?'

'No one,' replied Billy innocently. 'I was just saying to myself how good this chicken is.'

'Well don't talk with your mouthful. And don't you ever use a plate?'

She took a plate out of the cupboard and put it on the table in front of him.

'There,' she said, 'that wasn't so hard, was it?'

Believe it or not, Phillipa Slipper was in a good mood. She was always in a good mood after her course. 'Do you know what I learnt this evening?' she twittered excitedly. 'How to kill butterflies. Do you know the best way to kill a butterfly?' She didn't wait for an answer. 'You could try a fly swatter, but that might leave a terrible mark on the wall. So you can either suck them out of the air with a vacuum cleaner, or if that doesn't work, try catching them in a jar, put the lid on and watch them suffocate. Simple! And no mess. Ladybirds on the other hand . . .' Suddenly she stopped. She was looking directly at the lump under the tea towel. 'What . . . is . . . THAT, Billy Slipper?'

When his mother used his whole name Billy knew he was in trouble. He looked down at the chair. One of the cat's legs had popped out from beneath the tea towel.

'Um. It's just some project for school,' said Billy, getting up. 'It's not important. I was about to take it outside.'

'Don't you move a muscle,' she hissed.

Without taking her eyes off the tea towel, she reached into a drawer and took out a pair of kitchen tongs.

'If that is what I think it is, you are in big trouble, Billy Slipper. You know the rule about animals in my house.'

She lowered the tongs over the tea towel, gripped a corner and then, with a flick of the wrist, whisked it away.

Sometimes it feels like time stands still.

Nobody moved. The cat stared at Phillipa Slipper. A wide-eyed Phillipa Slipper stared at the cat and Billy . . . well, Billy shut his eyes and waited for the inevitable scream. And waited. And waited. Here it comes . . .

'AARRRGGGGHH!'

There it is.

Phillipa Slipper jumped back so high that she landed right in the kitchen sink. Her wriggling bottom caught against the cold tap, turning it on full blast.

'What is it? What's it doing in my house?' she wailed.

She tried lifting herself out of the sink, but she was stuck. Wedged in tight. Icy water poured down her back and all around the draining board. In the commotion, the cat panicked and fell off the chair. It scrabbled around helplessly, trying its best to stand up.

Mindy rushed into the kitchen. 'What's happened? Why did you scream?'

Then she saw the cat.

Wait for it. Wait for it. Here it comes . . .

'AARRRGGGGHH!'

There it is.

Mindy grabbed the broom from behind the

kitchen door and started jabbing it at the cat.

'Get out. Get out.'

'No, Mindy! Stop it!' cried Billy.

From the kitchen sink, Phillipa Slipper shouted encouragement to her daughter. 'Go on Mindy. Get it! Jab it! KILL IT!'

Tap water cascaded down the front of the cupboards, forming puddles on the plastic-covered floor. Phillipa Slipper tried to turn off the tap, frantically waving her arms around behind her, but she couldn't reach. In front of her eyes her kitchen was turning into one giant paddling pool.

Christopher Slipper appeared at the doorway wearing his pyjamas. You'd expect at a time like this that he'd say something, anything, but no, he just stood there rubbing his eyes in disbelief.

'Don't just stand there, you useless man. Do something!' bellowed his wife.

As Christopher Slipper waded over to the sink, Billy got hold of the broom and yanked it out of Mindy's hands. She slipped and splashed headfirst onto the sodden floor.

'I'm soaked,' she wailed. 'My hair!'

Quick as a shot, Billy grabbed the cat and for the second time that day, sprinted out of the house.

CHAPTER 4

MANDIDDEEITUS

The first time Billy ever met Mrs Mandiddee, he was in the garden trying to work out what kind of jam would cause the best traffic jam (strawberry, obviously), when suddenly, out of nowhere, he heard, 'Pssst.'

He looked around. Nothing.

'Pssst.'

This time, next to the rose bush, he saw an old woman, peering over the fence.

'Hey, you, come here,' she commanded.

Billy was a little scared. He'd heard about Mrs Mandiddee but this was the first time he'd ever seen her. Rumour had it she was a witch who only came out at night to boil badgers' heads.

Others thought she was a poisoner who'd escaped from a lunatic asylum. Sometimes, the children on the street played a game called, One Two Three Mandiddee, which was like Chase, except if you got caught you got Mandiddeeitus, a terrible disease that turned your arms and legs to jelly. Billy used to play it too, but that was before he had actually met Mrs Mandiddee.

'I've got something to show you,' she said.

Ever so slowly, Billy went over to the rose bush.

'What do you think of this?'

She reached over the fence and handed him a banana. And then, with a giggle, she was gone. His first thought, in keeping with the terrible rumours, was that the banana must be poisoned. Suspiciously, he turned it over in his hands. On the inside curve, he saw a funny face made up entirely by the black splodges a banana gets when it's old. The face was sticking out a long tongue, which snaked all the way up to the top. It really was the most peculiar banana Billy had ever seen.

From that day on, Billy and Mrs Mandiddee regularly exchanged gifts over the garden fence. He gave her a stick that looked like an enormous nose. He called it 'the sniffing stick'. She gave him

a handkerchief that once belonged to a Polish highwayman. He gave her a green, speckled eggshell he'd found in the woods. And so it went on until two weeks later, Billy plucked up his courage and knocked on her door. They quickly became the best of friends. Of course the other children in the street, especially Mindy, thought he'd gone mad and probably had Mandiddeeitus too. But Billy didn't care because no one made him as happy as Mrs Mandiddee did.

And now he stood on her doorstep once again, this time holding a soggy, jumbled-up cat under his arm.

'Come in, come in,' she said when she finally opened the door. 'Oh my heavens, what have you found this time? Bring it into the living room, the light's better in there.'

'Sounds like you're in a bit of bother,' said Mrs Mandiddee as she brought through a tray of tea and Bourbons from the kitchen. Her hands shook a little (well, she was over ninety years old), so as usual, most of the tea had splashed onto the tray. But she always insisted on doing it herself. She sat down on the sofa next to the cat.

'Oh my, what a beautiful creature it is.'

She stroked its belly and one by one gave all its legs a little squeeze, like a nurse checking a patient for broken bones.

'And you say it talks?' she asked.

'Sometimes,' replied Billy. 'And it can be quite rude too.'

There are not many adults in the world who would listen if you told them that your cat could talk. In fact, most of them would tell you not to be silly, that there's no such thing as a talking cat, and send you to bed with some disgusting medicine. But Mrs Mandiddee was different. She got off the sofa and knelt down on the floor in front of the cat.

'What's your name, little rudey puss?' she asked.

Since arriving at her house, the cat hadn't said a word. Most likely it was still in shock after meeting Billy's family for the first time. It stared inquisitively at Mrs Mandiddee and then, at last, it spoke.

'Your eyebrows look like hairy slugs.'

Mrs Mandiddee thought this was hilarious. She laughed and clapped her hands with joy.

'You're right! My eyebrows do look like hairy slugs. And my nose is huge, the size of a ripe old pear. But you still haven't told me your name.'

'I don't know what my name is,' replied the cat indifferently.

'Well, let's take a look at you and see what we can come up with,' said Mrs Mandiddee. 'You're furry and feisty . . . um, how about Feistypuss? No, no, no, that's no good; sounds like a Roman emperor with smelly armpits. What about Twisted Kitty? Oh, that's terrible. Muddlecat? Kitty Chitter Chatter? Help me, Billy.'

'How about Jumblecat?' suggested Billy.

'Brilliant,' said Mrs Mandiddee. She turned to the cat. 'Do you like Jumblecat?'

The cat rolled his eyes as if he was surrounded by the world's biggest idiots. 'Whatever. Just give me a biscuit.'

Mrs Mandiddee looked delighted. 'This cat is *so* rude. Wonderful! Billy, a biscuit for Jumblecat, please.'

Six biscuits later and Jumblecat was fast asleep.

Mrs Mandiddee agreed that Jumblecat should stay with her until they worked out a proper plan. Sometimes Billy wished he could stay with her too. He loved it at her house. It was like a museum. Not a boring museum full of glass cabinets and 'Do

Not Touch' signs, but a museum full of wonderful things that Billy was allowed to play with. Every inch of Mrs Mandiddee's house was crammed with paintings and ornaments and exotic bric-a-brac. When she was young, Mrs Mandiddee had travelled the world collecting souvenirs wherever she went, like the Iranian teapot with eight spouts or the set of tiny guitars made for Mexican fleas. She had an old German piano decorated with painted mice dancing in lederhosen and a cheese grater made of crocodile gut that she'd bought in Australia. Also, she had five sisters who lived all over the world and they sent her things too. Only last week her sister in South America had sent her a jar of Bolivian honey fish. At first it looked like a normal jar of honey, but when you held it up to the light you could see dozens of tiny, silver fish, lazily swimming around and around.

'Apparently,' said Mrs Mandiddee, reading the accompanying letter, 'they live happily in the honey for fifty years, as long as you keep them out of direct sunlight.'

Carefully, Billy put the honey fish on a shady shelf next to the sniffing stick.

But now they had Jumblecat to consider. Billy and

Mrs Mandiddee sat on the sofa with the sleeping cat in between them, and thought about what to do next.

'We could take Jumblecat to a vet,' suggested Billy. 'There must be an operation they can do to put everything back in the right place.'

Mrs Mandiddee stroked Jumblecat's soft belly. (Or was it his back? It was hard to tell what was what.)

'We'd need a lot of money to pay the vet's bills. How much have you got?'

'Millions and millions,' said Billy, smiling.

'Me too!' she giggled. 'The Mandiddee Millionaire. That's me!'

'I'm so rich, my toothbrush is made of gold.'

'Well, I'm so rich I use diamonds instead of sugar.' And to prove it, she poured a huge spoonful of sugar into her tea.

Of course, neither of them had a bean. Not a penny.

'Maybe I could sell some of my things,' said Mrs Mandiddee, looking around her busy living room.

'I could wash cars,' suggested Billy.

'What a good idea. We'd need some buckets and sponges. Twenty pence per car. Ten cars a day. That's two pounds a day. Oh dear, that's not very much, is it. Maybe thirty pence a car. We could call ourselves, "The Jumblecat Car Washing Company". I wonder where my wellies are?'

'And I could get a newspaper round as well.'

Suddenly Mrs Mandiddee sat bolt upright and stared at Billy. Her eyes sparkled like sugary diamonds.

'Newspaper!' she shrieked. 'That's it! The newspaper! Where's that newspaper?'

She leapt up off the sofa and hurried through to the kitchen as fast as her ninety-four-year-old legs would take her. From a cupboard under the sink, she pulled out an old newspaper and put it on the table.

'Now where was it? I'm sure it was in here. Not this page, not this page. Oh bother, it must be here somewhere. Wait a minute. Here it is.'

She pointed at the corner of the page.

'Read that, Billy. I haven't got my glasses handy.'

Billy began reading, rather puzzled. '"Missing boy found alive in microwave."'

'No, not that one, silly,' laughed Mrs Mandiddee. 'The one underneath.'

Tucked away at the bottom of the page was a small advert, the size of a matchbox.

DO YOU OWN AN UNUSUAL OR
TALENTED PET?
WOULD YOU LIKE TO WIN £10,000
AND A SASH?
THEN BRING YOUR PET TO:
'THE WORLD FAIR OF CURIOUS
CREATURES
AND STRANGE ANIMALS'
AT THE OLD GRAND HALL THIS
SUNDAY
£5 ENTRY PER ANIMAL
NO CROCODILES (EXCEPT THE
TOOTHLESS VARIETY)

Billy looked up at Mrs Mandiddee. 'It's in five days' time,' he said excitedly.

'Exactly,' replied Mrs Mandiddee, smiling an enormous, gap-toothed grin.

'We could win.'

'Exactly,' she said again.

'And pay for a vet to fix Jumblecat.'

'Exactly,' she said a third time.

'I'm so happy I could . . .'

'Dance?'

And so they jigged and jived and giggled their

way around the kitchen and into the living room. Lazily, Jumblecat opened one eye and watched them as they shimmied past the sofa.

'It's the Jumblecat Jive,' explained Mrs Mandiddee.

'It looks stupid, whatever it is,' said Jumblecat.

It was still an extremely rude cat.

CHAPTER 5

GROUNDED

Phillipa Slipper was angry. Furious! So blood-boilingly livid that when Billy squelched-scrunched into the kitchen later that evening she could hardly get her words out.

'Where is that . . . creature?'

'It ran away,' lied Billy.

He didn't want her to know that Jumblecat was staying with Mrs Mandiddee. Phillipa Slipper despised Mrs Mandiddee. She called her, among other things, 'that dirty old bag lady next door'.

'I'm sorry about the mess,' Billy said, trying to make things a little better.

Perhaps he should have kept his mouth shut.

'Mess! You call this a mess?' she wailed,

gesturing around her.

There were still pools of water on the floor, overturned chairs and even a half-eaten chicken drumstick floating about under the table. Billy's mum stood barefoot in the middle of it all with her trousers rolled up to her knees. She squeezed out the mop into a bucket.

'This isn't a mess, Billy Slipper, it's . . . it's . . . a catastrophe. You bring a hideous animal into my house, flood my kitchen and . . . and . . . you're a stupid, horrible, selfish boy. Why you can't be more like your sister, I don't know. Go to your room. You're grounded.'

'But . . .'

'No buts.'

'Until when?'

'Until I say so.'

'But there's somewhere I've to go this Sunday,' he pleaded. 'It's really important. Please, please, please. I'll do anything. I'll help you clean up. Look.'

Billy took a cloth from the sink and started mopping up water, squeezing it out into the bucket. Phillipa Slipper began to laugh. Not a real laugh. Apart from the time when the local pet shop burnt down, she never really laughed at all. Hers was the kind of laugh you hear in films when the mad queen decides to take over the world.

'Oh, you're funny, Billy Slipper,' she cackled, 'very funny indeed. Because if you think for one minute that this will make the slightest difference, then you are more stupid than I realised. You are grounded until this Sunday, and the next Sunday and the Sunday after that and for as many Sundays as I can count on my thumbs. Now get out of my sight.'

There was nothing he could do. Phillipa Slipper never changed her mind. Billy squelched out of the kitchen and up the stairs into his bedroom. He should have guessed that Mindy would be waiting for him. She loved it when her brother was in the doghouse.

'You're in trouble. You're in trouble,' she sang happily as soon as he came in. 'Anyhow, serves you right for calling me moose face.'

Billy ignored her. He'd just had the most incredible day of his life and now it was all ruined. Listening to Mindy harping on was the last thing he needed. Without getting undressed, he got into bed and pulled the covers up to his ears.

'What was that thing anyhow?' asked Mindy. 'It was disgusting.'

'He's called Jumblecat,' said Billy, pulling the pillow over his head. And he turned over and closed his eyes.

CHAPTER 6

A BRIEF HISTORY OF BAROMETERS

Over the next few days Billy's mother made sure he had plenty to do. On Wednesday he cleaned the bathroom from top to bottom using cotton buds, 'Because they get right into the corners like nothing else,' she explained. 'And don't forget to do inside the toilet. I'll be inspecting it later. You can be sure of that.'

He spent Thursday on his hands and knees, sucking up dust off the bedroom carpets using nothing more than a drinking straw, and on Friday he held the ladder steady as his mother covered the downstairs ceilings in plastic sheeting. Billy was getting desperate. Somehow he had to contact Mrs Mandiddee and let her know what was happening. He thought about ringing her, but every time he went near the telephone, his mother would suddenly appear from nowhere, as if she knew he was up to no good. (How do mothers do that?) But his biggest problem was that he wasn't allowed out of the house, not even for a moment, and his mother made sure of it.

On Saturday, Phillipa Slipper decided to take Mindy shopping. The summer sales were on and Phillipa Slipper loved a bargain. Christopher Slipper was, of course, expected to drive them into town and carry the bags. Before they set off she went around the whole house checking and double-checking that every window was closed and locked. There was no way Billy would be leaving the house while they were out. Then she unplugged the telephone and put it in her handbag.

'Now get to work,' she called, slamming the front door behind her.

He was trapped. A prisoner in his own home. It crossed his mind to jump through a downstairs window like in some of the cowboy films he'd seen, but he was in enough trouble already and anyhow, it would probably really hurt.

So, as instructed, he took a cloth from the cupboard and began dusting his mother's collection of encyclopedias, page by page by page. At page seventy-eight, a fantastically dreary page devoted to the history of barometers, there was a knock at the door. Billy ignored it. The only people who knocked on a Saturday were either selling dishcloths or more encyclopedias.

There was another, more urgent knock. 'It's me,' called a familiar voice.

Billy ran to the front door. Peering through the letterbox was a pair of twinkling, smiley eyes.

'Mrs Mandiddee!' Billy yelped.

'What's going on? I haven't seen you for days.'

'I'm grounded. I'm not allowed out of the house. I'm completely locked in. How's Jumblecat?'

'He's getting ever so fat eating all my biscuits. He wouldn't touch the cat food I bought him. He said it smelt like mouse sick. Cheeky thing. Tell me, are you allowed out tomorrow for the World Fair of Curious Creatures?'

'I'm not allowed out for weeks,' said Billy sadly. 'You'll have to go without me.'

'But we can't go without you. We need you. Do you want me to have a chat with your mother?'

Billy tried to picture Mrs Mandiddee and his mother sitting together on the plastic-covered sofa, sharing tea and biscuits and having a cosy chat.

Quite impossible.

'I'm sorry Mrs M, it's all my fault. I never should have brought Jumblecat home. If I'd come straight round to yours, then none of this would have happened.'

'Don't be silly. Listen, I'll go to the competition and I'll make sure we win. And as soon as you're allowed out we'll go to the vet together. You'll not miss out on any of that, I promise.' She pushed her fingers through the letterbox and tickled Billy's nose. 'Don't worry, Billy, it'll be fine, you'll see.'

And off she went, shuffling back to her house as fast as her ninety-four-year-old legs could carry her. Billy sat down in the hallway with his back to the door. He felt earth-shatteringly, moon-crushingly disappointed, but there was nothing he could do. He trudged back to the kitchen table, back to page seventy-eight of the encyclopedia, back to the history of barometers and all their dull secrets.

The shopping trip hadn't been a success.

Phillipa Slipper slammed her handbag down on the table. 'What a complete waste of time.' She turned to her husband. 'Why I trust you to do anything, I don't know. You're no better than an empty-brained milk churn. You're a festering lump of mould. No, that's not true. Even a festering lump of mould actually does something. It festers. You don't even fester. You just . . . nothing.'

Apparently the car had broken down. By the time Christopher Slipper got it going again the shops were closed. No one was to blame, cars break down all the time, but Phillipa Slipper saw it differently.

'If you knew more about cars, like a proper man, then none of this would have happened.'

'Yeah, Dad,' moaned Mindy. 'Now we've missed all the bargains and I'm going to look like an idiot. I can't wear these same clothes forever. I'll end up looking like a tramp.'

'You want your daughter looking like an idiot

tramp? Is that what you want?' shrieked Phillipa Slipper.

Christopher Slipper opened his mouth, but no words came out. Not a sound.

She watched him, hands on hips. 'Nothing to say? Well, there's a surprise.'

'There's a surprise,' copied Mindy, hands on hips.

Billy wished his dad would say something to defend himself, but he didn't. He just quietly shuffled past them into the living room and switched on the television.

'Hopeless,' sighed Phillipa Slipper.

'Hopeless,' mimicked Mindy.

Phillipa Slipper clutched her head theatrically. 'I've got a headache. I'm going to bed.'

Mindy followed, clutching her head in the same melodramatic way.

Just another day in the Slipper household.

Billy sat at the kitchen table listening to the television in the living room. It was some programme about pets doing funny things; chickens doing somersaults or dogs playing with yo-yos, that sort of thing. He was just about to go upstairs himself when he noticed his mother's handbag on the table. And it was open. And her house keys were lying right there on the top.

Now I think you know Billy Slipper enough by now to know that he's not a bad boy. Mischievous and something of a daydreamer, but not a bad boy. He would never dream of opening his mother's handbag and stealing from it. But it was already open and the keys were resting right there in front of him. And if he nudged the table just a tiny bit, like that, then they might even fall out onto the table. And they did!

He had a choice; be a good boy, put the keys back in the handbag and hope his mother forgave him by the morning, *or* take the keys and begin a great adventure. It didn't take him long to decide.

CHAPTER 7

ESCAPE

Mindy was sleep talking again. Billy didn't mind being woken up, that wasn't the problem; it was *what* she talked about that made him grit his teeth and stick his fingers in his ears. Some nights she'd say just a few words, turn over and fall back to sleep. Other nights, like tonight, she would talk and talk and talk.

'Doesn't my hair look nice! Your hair's greasy. Mine's shiny. I like brushing it. And combing it. Brush-comb-brush-comb. Oh, twitter-dee-dee, my hair's so pretty.'

That's right – hair talk. Endless hair talk.

Billy looked at his watch. It was time. From the gap in the curtains he could see the first signs of dawn taking over from the night shift, black sky melting into rich, promising purple. Carefully, without any jangling, he slid his mother's keys out from underneath the pillow and put them in his trouser pocket. He'd gone to bed fully clothed. One less thing to do this morning.

Mindy was really ranting. 'I like plaits more than ponytails. Don't you? My shampoo is so expensive. Your shampoo's cheap. You're bald!'

In one easy movement he rolled out of bed and slipped his feet into his shoes. Then he filled his bed with cushions and pulled the duvet over them. It looked like he was still in bed, fast asleep. Genius. So far so good.

Quiet as a mouse he tiptoed out of the bedroom and down the stairs, carefully avoiding the third and seventh steps which he knew were creaky. But at the bottom he stopped. He'd forgotten about the plastic sheeting that stretched all along the hallway, right up to the front door. There was no way he could walk on it without waking up his mother. He sat down on the bottom step and had a think.

There were two possibilities:

1. Jump up, catch hold of the lampshade and swing like Tarzan over the plastic sheeting onto the doormat.

2. Cut a small hole in the plastic and slither silently like a worm underneath the sheeting.

Billy decided on the swinging lampshade. He'd seen Tarzan do it a thousand times (though not on a lampshade) so it couldn't be that hard. He took a deep breath, reached out towards the lampshade and bent his knees to jump . . .

Let me tell you now that if he'd jumped it would have been disastrous. He would have crashed to the floor, pulling down not only the lampshade but also the whole light fitting, leaving a big hole in the ceiling. His mother would have woken up, found her precious hallway smashed to bits and her less precious son underneath the debris. Billy would have been sent to live in the cellar for at least five years and fed on a meagre diet of bread and water, except on Christmas Day when he'd receive a festive bowl of boiled cabbage.

What happened next was a total surprise. Christopher Slipper, dressed in his pyjamas, appeared at the top of the stairs. And then, stranger still, he spoke!

'Billy!' he said in a loud whisper. 'Wait.' And with those two words, he scurried off.

Billy didn't know what was going on. It was strange enough hearing his dad speak, but why did he rush off like that? Had he gone to wake up Phillipa Slipper? He wouldn't, would he?

And then he heard the toilet flush.

Instinctively, Billy understood what was going on. His dad was making the noise so Billy could escape. A diversion! With the water still cascading around the toilet, Billy leapt onto the plastic sheeting and hurry-scrunched up to the front door. He wrenched the keys out of his pocket, unlocked the door and stepped outside. Just as the toilet gave its final gurgle, he closed the door. Click! He'd made it.

As he reached Mrs Mandiddee's house he looked back over his shoulder, half expecting to see his mother chasing after him with a spatula. But everything was still. Everything apart from the curtain falling back over the bathroom window, but Billy didn't notice that.

CHAPTER 8

AN IMMEDIATE IMPRESSION

The Old Grand Hall was a magnificent building. Around town it was affectionately known as the Jellyfish; the glass-domed roof looked very much like the transparent body of a jellyfish and the columns trailing below were like its delicate tentacles. Billy had passed it on the bus many times and barely paid it any attention, but this morning, for the first time, he saw just how extraordinary it was.

'I'm told it's taller than the Eiffel Tower and wider than the Amazon River,' exclaimed Mrs Mandiddee, squinting against the sun. (It was big, but not that big.) 'Apparently, if you climb to the top of the glass dome, on a clear day you can see Mount Everest.' (Actually, on a clear day you might be able to see

Tumbledown Hill, but that was about it.)

An enormous banner hung across the front of the Old Grand Hall. It read:

THE WORLD FAIR OF CURIOUS
CREATURES AND STRANGE ANIMALS
WELCOMES YOU.
PREPARE TO BE AMAZED.

Jumblecat was fast asleep inside an old, blue suitcase that Mrs Mandiddee had found in her attic. They'd drilled a few air holes in it and lined the inside with cushions. It was perfectly comfortable, but that didn't stop Jumblecat from complaining.

'In Ancient Egypt they worshipped the cat, not stuck him in some manky old suitcase.'

Mrs Mandiddee explained that they couldn't just carry him around on the bus as he was. People weren't used to seeing jumbled-up cats on buses.

'Well, if I'm to be cooped up in here, I demand a biscuit. No, make that three.'

Billy gave him three Bourbons, rearranged his legs and shut the lid.

Quite a crowd had gathered outside the Old Grand

Hall. Billy put down the suitcase and took a deep breath. He was starting to get nervous.

'If we win and there's any money left over, we should visit your sister in Bolivia.'

'What a great idea,' replied Mrs Mandiddee.

He looked up at his old friend. His stomach was turning with excitement. 'Do you think we might win?'

Mrs Mandiddee smiled one of her huge smiles. All the wrinkles seemed to fall off her face. She looked not a day over seventy-five. 'You know what, Billy, we just might.' She gave his hand a squeeze. 'Shall we go in?'

And so they did, Billy and Mrs Mandiddee hand in hand and Jumblecat sleeping among the cushions and biscuit crumbs inside the suitcase.

Jumblecat made an immediate impression.

'What on earth is *that*?' asked the spotty young man responsible for taking the five pounds entry fee. 'I've seen some strange things today, but this takes the biscuit.'

'He's called Jumblecat,' replied Mrs Mandiddee. 'And please keep your voice down, he's sleeping.' She handed him a bag of coins, mostly small change that she'd found down the back of her sofa.

'Jumblecat? It's a cat, is it? OK, if you say so.' He ran his finger down the list in front of him. 'Urmm, cats, cats . . . here it is. Aisle three, cats. When you get there look for someone wearing a yellow jacket, they'll tell you what to do. And you need to fill in this entry form; name and address, that sort of thing.' He looked quizzically at Jumblecat again. 'Are you sure it's a cat?'

'I'm sure,' replied Billy.

Billy filled in the form and returned it to the spotty young man. They were in.

The noise inside the main hall was incredible. What a racket! Hundreds of different animal sounds echoed throughout the enormous space. There were cluckings and barkings and bayings and neighings, all coming together in a deafening animal cacophony. And it didn't smell too good either. Billy held his nose and looked around. Above him, great shafts of sunlight flooded in through the glass-domed ceiling. He could see the outline of an aeroplane crossing the sky. For a strange moment he felt like he'd been swallowed alive by the Jellyfish and was wallowing around in its watery tummy. It all made him feel quite dizzy.

The animal enclosures were arranged alphabetically, aisle by aisle. Aisle one was aardvarks through to beavers. Aisle two was bees through to camels, and so on, all the way through to yaks and zebras in aisle twenty-three.

'Here we are,' said Mrs Mandiddee. She read out loud from the large sign. 'Aisle three; Caribou, Carp, Carpet Moths, Caterpillars, Catfish, Cats and Centipedes.'

They headed up aisle three, past a caribou munching from a trough full of grass. Three giant antlers sat on top of its head.

Billy stared at it for a while. 'Do caribous normally have three antlers?'

'I don't think so. It's an unusual caribou,' replied Mrs Mandiddee.

The caribou tried lifting its head, but the weight of the three antlers was too much. Its head slumped back into the trough. It wasn't much fun being an unusual caribou.

At the carp enclosure, Billy put his face up against the glass tank and peered into the murky water. Eventually, a carp swam lazily past.

'What's so unusual about that?' he asked. 'It looks like any old fish.'

'Look again, and listen this time,' said the carp's owner, a man with a face like an overinflated pink balloon.

The carp re-emerged out of the gloom and this time it sneezed; a muffled, watery 'A-tishoo!'

Billy jumped back.

'Fish don't sneeze,' he said to the man.

'This one can. Does it all the time. Sometimes six sneezes in a row.'

Mrs Mandiddee looked into a different tank. 'What does this one do?'

'Aaahh,' he said, bristling with pride. 'That's my star carp. Tell it a joke.'

'What do you mean, tell it a joke?' asked Mrs Mandiddee.

'Tell it a joke, simple,' insisted the man.

So Mrs Mandiddee told the fish a joke. It wasn't even a very funny joke, something about a bear eating too much cheese, but as the carp swam by, little bubbles of air escaped from its smiling mouth and a faint chuckling sound could be heard through the glass.

'That's nothing,' said the man. 'If you'd told it a half-decent joke it would have turned upside down and done a proper belly laugh.'

Mrs Mandiddee clapped her hands with joy. 'It's wonderful! A laughing carp! Whatever next!'

Whatever next indeed. As they wandered up aisle three they saw dancing carpet moths, caterpillars jumping over matchstick fences and most impressively, a catfish that leapt out of its tank through a hoop of fire.

The cat enclosure was the largest of them all. There were cats everywhere; some still in their travel boxes, some wandering around on the floor and others squatting on tall perches next to their owners. At first glance Billy couldn't see much that was unusual about any of these cats; there was one with slightly pinkish fur and another with huge bushy whiskers, but none of them seemed that out of the ordinary.

Billy spotted a tired-looking woman wearing a yellow jacket.

'Excuse me,' he said, 'we've come to register our cat in the competition.'

The woman didn't even look up from her clipboard. 'You're too late.'

'Too late?'

'We're full up. Too many cats.' She looked up at Billy. 'Can't you see? I've got cats coming out of my ears. People think they can just turn up with their precious moggy, dress it in something funny and they'll win the competition. It's ridiculous. Look!' She pointed at a cat wearing a knitted bonnet sitting on a perch near the front. Billy had to agree, it did look ridiculous. 'This is a competition for unusual or talented pets. The only talent these cats have is sitting on their furry bums and eating overpriced cat food. Why I was assigned cats I don't know. They could have given me something exciting like leopards or anteaters, but no, what did old muggins get? Cats.'

She was quite out of breath after her rant. Billy found her a chair to sit down on.

'Thank you,' she said breathily.

She tore off a piece of paper from her clipboard and gave it to Billy. 'Give that to the man at the front entrance and he'll refund your entry fee.'

'But . . .'

'No buts. I'm sure your cat is a lovely, pretty pussy, but we're full.'

But before Billy could take the piece of paper, Mrs Mandiddee thrust the suitcase onto the woman's lap, opened the latches and lifted the lid. The lady in the yellow jacket gasped.

'It's . . . it's . . . magnificent!'

Jumblecat squinted as his eyes adjusted to the bright light.

'Truly magnificent. May I touch it?'

'Of course you can,' said Billy, turning to smile at Mrs Mandiddee. 'He's called Jumblecat.'

'Jumblecat,' cooed the lady. 'I'm sure we can squeeze you in somewhere.'

CHAPTER 9

COLONEL BEAUVRILLE

You never forget the first time you see Colonel Charles Beauvrille. You see, he's huge. Imagine the tallest, fattest man in the world and then double it. Triple it! If he was around in the time of fairy tales then he'd be the giant who waddles about, knocking things over and being a general nuisance.

'Who's that?' Billy asked the lady in the yellow jacket.

'That's Colonel Beauvrille,' she replied, breathless with excitement. She stood up from her chair and began brushing cat hairs off her skirt. 'This is *his* competition. He started it. He pays for it. He chooses the winner and he donates the prize money. And the sash. They say he's one of the richest men in the country.'

'He's enormous,' said Mrs Mandiddee, rather stating the obvious, but what else could you say?

They all stared as Colonel Beauvrille waddled up aisle three. He truly was a giant of a man with a thick black beard and huge meaty hands. He wore tweed from top to toe: a tweed cap, a tweed jacket, tweed plus fours, which are like trousers that have shrunk in the wash because they stop just below the knees, tweed socks (which must have been very itchy) and shoes with a tweed design

sewn into the leather. He paused for a moment outside the caribou enclosure and whispered something to his assistant, who wore a yellowy green jumper that would embarrass a gooseberry. (Let's call him Mr Gooseberry.) Mr Gooseberry scribbled something in his notepad and together they continued up aisle three.

By the time they reached the cat enclosure, Colonel Beauvrille was sweating profusely. He took a tweed handkerchief out of his pocket and mopped his brow.

'What have we got here, then?' he said, casting his eye over the clutter of cats.

'Cats,' replied Mr Gooseberry. As you can see, he was a very useful assistant.

'Any unusual cats? What about that one?' He pointed at the cat wearing a bonnet. 'Is that your cat, madam?'

'Yes,' replied the lady, 'I knitted it myself.'

'You knitted the cat?' Colonel Beauvrille burst into a curiously high-pitched giggle that was entirely unsuited to a man of his size. 'Oh my! Hilarious! Well, I think we've seen everything there is to see here. Thank you all for coming. The finalists will be announced shortly.' He turned to Mr Gooseberry and whispered, 'Pathetic. Absolutely pathetic. Cats always are. What's next?'

Mr Gooseberry looked at his notepad. 'Centipedes.'

'Centipedes. No doubt there'll be one with only ninety-nine legs. Just like last year. Let's go.' And that was that. He turned and waddled off.

Billy was furious. He felt cheated. He hadn't come all this way for nothing. 'Excuse me, Mr Beauvrille,' he shouted.

Colonel Beauvrille stopped but didn't turn around. 'My name is *Colonel* Beauvrille.'

'I'm sorry. Colonel Beauvrille. I don't think you saw my cat.'

He still had his back to Billy. 'And what makes your cat so special? Let me guess, you've dressed it up as a baby. Stuck a dummy in its mouth and put a nappy on it?' He giggled again, but somehow he sounded angry at the same time. 'I don't think you understand what this competition is all about.'

Billy pointed at Jumblecat. 'That's my cat.'

With an impatient snort, Colonel Beauvrille turned and looked at the old, blue suitcase. He froze. A single pearl of sweat rolled down his forehead and dangled off the end of his nose. For a moment he looked like he was about to cry. But he didn't say a word. Not to Billy, not to anyone. And then, as if nothing had happened, he just turned on his heels and waddled off in the direction of the centipedes, with Mr Gooseberry trotting close behind.

CHAPTER 10

MINDY'S RAISIN FACE

Mr Gooseberry stepped onto the stage and tapped the microphone. 'Ladies and gentlemen,' he bellowed. 'Your attention please. After careful consideration and deliberation, I have here, in this envelope, the names of the finalists as chosen by Colonel Charles Beauvrille.'

Billy felt a terrible sinking feeling in his stomach. After all, Colonel Beauvrille had barely glanced at Jumblecat. He looked up at Mrs Mandiddee. She was biting her fingernails. Jumblecat was snoring peacefully in the suitcase.

Mr Gooseberry opened the envelope. 'The eight finalists are . . . the knitting monkey; the fast snail; the blushing rabbit;' (apparently it blushed if you said, 'smelly socks') 'the firefly beetle; the tiny hippopotamus;' (it was no bigger than a hairbrush) 'the somersaulting kangaroo; the barking goose and the jumbled-up cat known as Jumblecat. Will all the finalists join me on the stage, please.'

Billy punched the air with joy. Mrs Mandiddee shrieked and Jumblecat continued snoring. The lady in the yellow jacket was just as excited. She grabbed Billy, spun him round in the air and gave him a big, soggy kiss on his cheek.

'You go up there and win,' she said, squeezing half the life out of him. 'That cat is something special.'

'I'll do my best,' wheezed Billy.

She put him down and ruffled his hair. Normally Billy hated having his hair ruffled, but just now, he didn't mind one little bit.

He closed the suitcase lid and headed up to the stage with Mrs Mandiddee and the seven other finalists.

Now, I know this is Billy's story and today is Billy's big day, but something was happening at home that I have to tell you about, something that would change everything.

It all started because Mindy was bored. There are few things as venomous, few things quite as explosive as a bored Mindy. When Mindy was bored her bottom lip stuck right out and her eyes narrowed into angry little squints as if two raisins had been squashed on her face in place of her eyes. If there ever was a family joke among the Slippers, then it was 'Mindy's raisin face'. But it's not even that funny and besides, the Slippers didn't do family jokes.

Mindy stomped into her bedroom. 'I'm bored.'

She threw a shoe at the Billy-shaped lump under the duvet.

'I'm bored,' she said again, louder this time.

She waited for a reaction. When none came she picked out her least favourite doll from under her bed, a bald, ugly thing she called Farchy Stinkton, and stomped downstairs. They had a tea party, but Farchy Stinkton forgot to say thank you so had to be punished. The poor doll was stripped and put in the washing machine on a cool cycle. For a while Mindy was content to watch Farchy Stinkton spin round and round, but not for long.

She stomped into the living room. 'I'm bored.'

Christopher Slipper was watching television, a quiz show about vegetables. Mindy snatched the remote control out of his hand and began flicking through the channels.

Flick. 'Boring.' Flick. 'Boring.' Flick. 'Double boring.' Flick.

And then, just as she was about to throw the remote control back at her dad, she saw something that made her raisin eyes open wide in disbelief.

'MUM!' she bellowed. 'BILLY'S ON TV!'

There he was, live, on stage at the Old Grand Hall with Jumblecat.

Phillipa Slipper came into the room holding a feather duster and wearing a mask over her mouth.

'Look, Mum. Billy's on TV. I want to be on TV.'

'Don't be silly, Mindy. He can't be on TV. You said he was in bed.'

'He is in bed. I think,' said Mindy.

Christopher Slipper blushed, just a little, but of course nobody noticed him.

Mindy stamped her foot on the plastic sheeting. 'S'not fair. I should be on TV. I'm three minutes older than him. I wash my hair every day. Mum, get me on TV.'

But Phillipa Slipper ignored her. She was pointing furiously at the television. 'Look. He's with that thing, that – that disgusting creature that ruined my kitchen. He told me it had run away. He lied to me! And look! There's that geriatric bag lady from next door. What's going on?' She growled at the television like an angry dog.

'Quick, turn up the sound,' Mindy barked at her dad.

At last Christopher Slipper spoke. 'But you've got the remote . . .'

'Sssshhh,' Mindy hissed, pointing the remote control at the television. 'I'm listening.'

* * *

'So, Mr Billy Slipper, how does it feel to be in the finals of the World Fair of Curious Creatures and Strange Animals?'

Mr Gooseberry thrust the microphone so close to Billy's face he could feel it tickling the hairs in his nose. Behind Mr Gooseberry, a television cameraman pointed his camera directly at Billy.

'It feels, um, great. I'm very happy.'

'And tell us a little bit about your cat.'

'He's called Jumblecat and he likes biscuits and chicken drumsticks and . . .'

'Fascinating,' interrupted Mr Gooseberry. 'And what will your cat be performing for us this afternoon?'

'Performing?' asked Billy. 'What do you mean?'

This was the first Billy had heard about any performance. Mr Gooseberry impatiently explained that each finalist was expected to give some kind of performance, a demonstration of their talent.

'Did you read the rules?' he asked. 'No?'

'No,' said Billy quietly. He heard some people sniggering in the audience. At home, Mindy almost fell off the sofa, laughing. There was nothing quite as funny as seeing her twin brother humiliated. And on live television too.

Mr Gooseberry tutted like an exasperated teacher.
'Well, if you don't read the rules . . .' and off he went
to interview the owner of the tiny hippo.

'What are we going to do?' Billy asked Mrs
Mandiddee.

Mrs Mandiddee looked far from worried. In fact,
she had a twinkle in her eye. 'Don't worry, Billy. I
know what to do.'

'But we need to do something.' He was getting
panicky. 'What are we going to do?'

She pointed at a piano at the far side of the stage.
'You'll see,' she said with a smile. And that was all
she would say on the matter.

CHAPTER 11

THE PERFORMANCE

Colonel Beauvrille loved making an entrance.

Bagpipers, forty of them, marched onto the stage, deafening the crowd with their Highland wail. They were joined by forty drummers, followed by a choir of children who did their best to be heard above the racket. Each bagpiper, drummer and child was dressed top to toe in tweed and wore false black beards. It looked like there were a hundred Colonel Beauvrilles of varying sizes parading around the stage. Just as the noise reached fever pitch, a trapdoor opened centre stage and through it rose the massive man himself, Colonel Beauvrille, seated on an enormous throne. He waved like royalty at the bemused crowd and pretended to wipe away tears with his tweed handkerchief, as if he was overcome by the emotion of the occasion. When at last he was settled, he nodded at Mr Gooseberry, signalling that he was ready for the performances to begin.

'Our first performance this afternoon comes from an animal of extraordinary talent, an animal so unique –'

'Get on with it,' interrupted Colonel Beauvrille.

'Ladies and gentlemen, the knitting monkey.'

And what a knitter it was! The monkey picked up two knitting needles and a ball of wool and off it went. Within a minute it had completed a scarf. After two minutes it had made a hat, complete with a bobble. The crowd hooted with delight.

The firefly beetle was next and just as impressive. As the lights dimmed, great flashes of colour exploded out of the tiny insect; streaks of red and yellow and green spilling out over the heads of the crowd. It was quite a show.

There followed the rabbit that blushed, the goose that barked and the tiny hippo that dived off a small platform into a glass of milk. The fast snail was strapped onto a tiny roller-skate and rolled down a ramp (bit of a cheat, thought Billy), and the somersaulting kangaroo got stage fright and hopped off behind the curtain. That only left Jumblecat.

Billy turned to Mrs Mandiddee. 'What shall I do?'

'Nothing. Nothing at all.'

'But Jumblecat's still sleeping. Shall I wake him up?'

'No, let him sleep.' Gently, she squeezed his shoulder. 'It'll be OK, Billy. Just watch.' And with that, Mrs Mandiddee took a seat at the piano on the far side of the stage.

As the crowd hushed, a spotlight shone on the sleeping cat. Only his gentle snores disturbed the silence.

Mrs Mandiddee began to play an old tune that Billy recognised straight away. She'd played it to him dozens of times before when he was round her house. But why now? He looked over at Jumblecat. Nothing was happening. He was still fast asleep.

'Wake up, Jumblecat,' he said under his breath. 'Do something. Please.'

And at that very moment, Jumblecat's ears started to twitch. And then, slowly, his head rose up from the cushion and began to sway rhythmically from side to side. His eyes were still closed. He seemed to be in some kind of trance, hypnotised by the music.

And then, inexplicably, Jumblecat began to sing.

The purest, sweetest sound came out of his mouth. No words, just melodious miaows that floated around the Old Grand Hall. Billy was as shocked as everyone else. Even Mindy, watching the television at home, stopped moaning and listened in enthralled silence. It was incredible. Beautiful! A shiver of pleasure travelled up Billy's spine. He looked over at Colonel Beauvrille. The giant man was crying.

As Mrs Mandiddee played the last few notes, Jumblecat's head rolled gently back down onto the cushion and as if nothing had happened, he started snoring once again.

With his face streaked with tears, Colonel Beauvrille got up from his throne and waddled over to Billy. 'The winner,' he proclaimed. He took hold of Billy's arm and raised it into the air. 'Jumblecat is the winner.'

The rest of the afternoon passed in a great blur of happiness. Billy was presented with a briefcase bulging with prize money. Cameras flashed and reporters asked question after question. What did he plan to do with the money? Where did Jumblecat come from? Was Mrs Mandiddee his granny? His great-granny? He waved at the audience and they waved back. The bearded bagpipers piped and the bearded children sang. It was sensational. The best moment of his life.

Though there was one strange thing that happened. As the smiling Colonel Beauvrille placed the winner's sash over Billy's head, he leant down and whispered, 'How much for the cat?'

'Oh, thank you, but he's not for sale,' replied Billy. 'I'm keeping him.'

The smile never left Colonel Beauvrille's face. Not for a second. But there was no mistaking the giant man's eyes momentarily bulging with fury.

'It doesn't matter,' said Colonel Beauvrille. He put his arm around Billy's shoulders and squeezed a little too hard. 'Now smile for the cameras.'

CHAPTER 12

FAT-NOSED LOON

If you like normal, happy endings, close the book now. That's right, off you go! You can tell yourself that Jumblecat went to the vet and had a successful operation. With the money left over, Billy, Mrs Mandiddee and not-so-jumbled-up Jumblecat went on holiday to visit her sister in Bolivia. And that's it. There's your happy ending.

But if you want to know what really happened, you'd better keep reading.

Still here?

Good.

Billy felt ten feet tall. His mouth ached from smiling so much. Complete strangers approached and congratulated him, shaking him enthusiastically by the hand. As he stepped outside into the evening sun he became aware that everything around him looked different; brighter, shinier, *better*. Even the trees looked greener than they had this morning. He looked down at the winner's sash that hung across his body. Apart from a second-hand bread bin at a school raffle, Billy had never won anything in his life before. Nothing. Things like this didn't happen to boys like him. Only now was the reality beginning to sink in . . . They'd WON! A ridiculous, HUMONGOUS amount of money. More than enough to get Jumblecat fixed. And maybe there'd be enough left over for a holiday to Bolivia to see Mrs Mandiddee's sister. (See! Even Billy believes in normal happy endings. Silly Billy!)

'How did you know that Jumblecat could sing?' Billy asked as they got on the bus to take them home.

'It was pure luck,' answered Mrs Mandiddee. 'That first evening, after you'd left Jumblecat at my house, I started playing the piano. Next thing I know, he's singing. I thought it was the kettle boiling or foxes wailing in the garden, but it was him, singing in his sleep. The same thing happened the next evening and the next. So when I saw the piano in the Old Grand Hall I knew everything was going to be all right.' She patted the suitcase on the seat in between them. 'It's hard to believe something so rude and jumbled up can sing so beautifully. I don't think even he knows he can sing like that.'

'Well, it's because of you we won. Thank you, Mrs M.'

She smiled a tired smile and gave his hand a gentle squeeze. As the bus pulled away, Billy looked back at the Old Grand Hall. The lazy evening sun shimmered over the glass-domed roof, around which dozens of swallows swooped and dive-bombed, swerving away at the last second.

'Let me out!' demanded a cross voice from inside the suitcase.

Billy opened the lid. Two of Jumblecat's legs uncurled and stretched towards the roof of the bus. 'Did I win? Even if I came last, which I very much doubt, I am never travelling inside this suitcase again. And no more buses; it's so embarrassing.'

Billy smiled at this extraordinary, cantankerous creature sprawled among the cushions. 'You did it, Jumblecat. You won!'

'Of course I won. Did you see the other cats? What an ugly bunch. I bet they all drink from the toilet. Anyhow, where's my half?'

'Half of what?' asked Mrs Mandiddee.

'Half of the prize money, you wombat! I've got big plans. First of all I want proper food, none of that cheap muck you've been giving me. We'll hire a chef. And then you've got to redecorate the spare room. I can't move in there until you get rid of that disgusting wallpaper. It must be well over a hundred years old, just like you.'

Mrs Mandiddee giggled and raised her hands in mock horror. 'I'm only ninety-four, you cheeky thing.'

But Jumblecat wasn't finished yet. 'And your sofa's too itchy, so we'll need to replace that. And then I want grooming once a week by a professional. I'm not having one of you two coming near me with a pair of scissors. Look at you both!' He waved a paw at Billy's head. 'Who cuts your hair?'

'My mother,' answered Billy.

'That fat-nosed loon. Well, that explains it. Tell her that wonky pudding-bowl haircuts went out with the dinosaurs.'

'I will.' Billy grinned.

It was good to see that success hadn't changed Jumblecat in the slightest.

CHAPTER 13

THE PARTY

Something wasn't right. Billy put down the suitcase and rubbed his eyes. Maybe it was some kind of mirage, a trick of the evening light.

Mrs Mandiddee squinted down the road. 'Isn't that your sister?'

It was no mirage. There was Mindy, standing outside their house, and she was waving and *smiling*. She never waved at him and certainly never smiled. She must be waving at someone else, he thought, and glanced over his shoulder. But nobody else was around. As they got closer, Billy saw a homemade banner stretched across the front of the house. In big colourful letters, it read:

CONGRATULATIONS BIL

Mindy ran ahead to meet them. 'We saw you on TV. It was amaaazing. Mum says you can keep the cat. I've made a bed for it in the shed. Is this your sash? Can I touch it?' She danced around him, clapping her hands. 'You looked a bit funny on television but it was brilllllliant. And the cat was brilllllliant! A singing cat! Brilllllliant! Where is it?'

Billy tapped the side of the suitcase. He was speechless. In all his life he had never seen his twin sister in such a good mood.

'Come on. Mum's waiting. And we've got a surprise for you inside,' she said, tugging at his sleeve.

Billy picked up the suitcase. 'Are you coming, Mrs M?'

Mrs Mandiddee shook her head. 'This old lady needs her beauty sleep.' She kissed him on the forehead. 'You go. Have fun.' And off she tottered back to her house.

Mindy could hardly get her words out fast enough. 'I made the banner all by myself. But I ran out of space on the paper to write your whole name. You don't mind, do you?'

'Of course not. It's great,' replied Billy, finally giving in to Mindy's persistent sleeve tugging.

* * *

'No peeking.'

Mindy put her hands over Billy's eyes and guided him along the hallway towards the kitchen.

'Are you ready? Three. Two. One. Ta-daaa!'

For a moment Billy thought he must be in the wrong house; that Mindy had taken him through a secret passage into a wonderful place. There were balloons tied to the walls, the lampshade was festooned with multicoloured streamers that stretched to each corner of the room and best of all, the kitchen table was piled high with the most delicious-looking goodies imaginable: jelly, crisps,

sausages, sweets and of course, biscuits. Towering over everything was a gigantic cake in the shape of . . . Billy took a closer look . . . in the shape of Jumblecat.

'I did the orange icing,' bragged Mindy. 'And his head is made of marzipan.'

There had never been a party in his house before. Normally Phillipa Slipper hated parties. In her mind, parties meant mess. Cakes might crumble, drinks might spill and worst of all, all those horrible children pinballing around her house with their sticky fingers and high-pitched squeals. Yuck! Once, when Billy was approaching his fifth birthday, he asked his mother if he could have a party. You know what she said?

'A party? Read my lips, Billy Slipper. There will never be a party in this house.' Four-year-old Billy couldn't lip-read, but he got the message anyhow.

True to her word, there were no birthday parties, Easter egg parties or even Christmas parties in her house. In fact, Christmas in the Slipper household was pretty much like any other day except for the plastic Christmas tree that stood solemnly in the corner of the living room without lights or baubles. On Boxing Day morning it was hurriedly wrapped in plastic and returned to the attic for another year.

Yet here it was. A party! In his house!

Phillipa Slipper came into the kitchen. She was wearing her best dress, the brown one with brown tassels on the sleeves. Billy hardly recognised her, not because of the dazzlingly dreary dress, but because she too was smiling.

'What do you think?' she asked, gesturing at the food and decorations.

'It's amazing. Thank you.'

In all his wildest dreams he never thought there'd be a moment like this.

Phillipa Slipper took a knife out of the kitchen drawer, removed it from its plastic sheath and handed it to Billy.

'Well, don't just stand there. Cut the cake!'

CHAPTER 14

A PERFECT DAY

Jumblecat wasn't so happy about sleeping in the shed; he'd got quite comfortable on Mrs Mandiddee's sofa, thank you very much. But Mindy had done her best and made it as cosy as could be, with plenty of blankets and cushions. Billy carried out two bowls, one for water and the other filled with a selection of broken biscuits left over from the party.

'Why do I have to sleep in the shed?' whinged Jumblecat as he tucked into a custard cream.

'You're lucky to be staying here at all. Just remember what happened last time I brought you home.'

Billy arranged the blankets around Jumblecat (not

as easy as it sounds – his legs kept popping out all over the place). 'Tomorrow I'll find a vet and you'll be good as new in no time. Goodnight, Jumblecat and thank you.'

'What for?'

'For being my friend.'

Jumblecat coughed, spraying tiny pieces of custard cream across the shed floor. 'You see, I told you I had a cough. I'm sure it's cat flu. And shut the door behind you – there's a terrible draught in here. Some friend! If I get pneumonia and die I'll haunt you forever.'

Billy smiled and closed the door. It was a warm, clear night and a thousand stars twinkled in the sky. And there! Yes! A shooting star shot through the darkness like a sparkling bullet. Making a wish wasn't as easy as he thought. Everything seemed just about perfect at the moment; even his mother was just how a mother should be.

As he headed back inside he could see her through the kitchen window doing the washing-up. He watched her as she scrubbed a plate, bringing it up to her face for a close inspection and plunging it back into the sink again for yet another more vigorous scrub. She hadn't once mentioned the stolen keys or his sneaking out of the house at the crack of dawn. In fact, she seemed genuinely happy for him.

'And when Jumblecat started singing, Oh, the tears ran down my face,' she had said. And then, 'When that Colonel announced Billy Slipper as the winner, my Billy, I could hardly contain myself, could I, Mindy.'

Apparently, she said, she started baking the cake that very moment. Mindy blew up the balloons and Christopher Slipper was sent out to the shops to get the other treats.

'My boy deserves a party,' she said to Billy and even ruffled his hair. (Of course, she washed her hands straight after.)

Billy looked up at the stars once more and made his wish. If it came true then he would be the happiest boy in the world.

'Now Billy Slipper,' he said to himself, 'one more slice of cake before bed can't hurt.' And he strode back inside to his family.

Billy lay in bed, rubbing his swollen tummy. He'd eaten so much he was in danger of exploding and showering his bedroom in cakey confetti. With a gentle groan, he rolled onto his side and reached under the bed. Tucked in among some of his Collectabillya, he felt for, and found the briefcase full of prize money. *Just checking*, he told himself. On her side of the room Mindy was fast asleep and tonight, to round off the day, she wasn't sleep-talking. It had been a perfect day; winning the competition and the unexpected party and to cap it all, being allowed to keep Jumblecat. At last, his very own pet. An irritable, overweight pet, but nonetheless, his.

CHAPTER 15

IT WAS ALL A TRICK

It's a curious time, that moment, just before you properly wake. Lingering, blancmange dreams mingle with the first sounds of the day, until, like a diver in a sea of sleep, you rise slowly to the surface. Billy heard mumbling voices, doors opening and closing. He couldn't be sure if he was awake or if he was still dreaming. He heard his mother talking to someone outside. Mindy perhaps? No, not Mindy. Not whiney enough. Who was it? It was certainly a voice he recognised. With great will he opened his eyes. And then it came to him . . .

'Colonel Beauvrille!' he said out loud, surprising himself with the volume of his own voice.

He sat up and listened. There it was again, that

curious high-pitched giggle that he'd heard for the first time only yesterday. Then a car started – an engine roaring into life. (It certainly wasn't the Slippers' family car, which choked and gurgled like an overfed baby.) Billy jumped out of bed and looked out of the window just in time to see the giant man ease himself into a black Rolls-Royce. Phillipa Slipper stood by the side of the car doing a series of strange little curtseys. Then, as elegantly as a swan, the magnificent vehicle reversed out of their driveway and glided off down the street.

How peculiar. Billy rubbed the sleep out of his eyes and tried to think. What was he doing here? How did Colonel Beauvrille even know where he lived? Then he remembered filling out the name and address form when he arrived at the Old Grand Hall. That would be it, he told himself. Perhaps Colonel Beauvrille had come to congratulate Billy personally, away from all the cameras. But then why didn't his mother wake him? The more he thought about it, the more he felt something wasn't quite right. He had an uneasy feeling in his tummy and this time it wasn't from eating too much cake.

He dressed and went downstairs. The kitchen was immaculate. All the balloons and streamers had gone and no leftover treats graced the table. It was as if the party had never happened. In the living room he saw Mindy pirouetting around the sofa, singing one of her made-up songs.

'It's so nice to be pretty, just like me. Tra la laaa.'

'Mindy, why was Colonel Beauvrille here?'

She ignored him and carried on singing. 'With hair like a mermaid and I smell like the sea. Tra la laaa.'

And then he noticed. She was wearing the sash. *His* sash! Which he had put in the briefcase under his bed along with the prize money. Things were starting to look very bad.

'Where did you get that from?' He could hear his voice shaking.

'What?' replied Mindy, sweet as anything.

'My sash. Where did you get it from?'

'Mummy gave it to me. She said I could keep it. Do you think I look pretty?'

He didn't answer. He ran back upstairs to his bedroom and looked under the bed.

It was gone. The money, the briefcase, all gone.

His mind was racing, trying to consider every possibility. Maybe his mother had moved it for safe keeping. Maybe Mindy had hidden it for a joke. Yes, that'd be it. It'd be just the sort of thing she'd do.

He crossed over the skipping rope into her side of the room and scanned the shelves full of her dolls, looking for a hiding place.

He didn't hear his sister come into the room. 'What are you doing on my side?'

'Where is it, Mindy? Where did you hide the money?'

'I haven't got it,' she said innocently.

Billy yanked a doll down from off the shelf, a talking doll called Harmony Happity Hapkins. He knew it was one of Mindy's favourites. 'Tell me or I promise I'll . . .'

Mindy didn't look at all worried about what Billy might do to her doll. In fact, calm as you like, she sat down at her dressing table and started combing her hair.

'You know the party yesterday. It was all a trick.' She was watching him in the mirror. 'It was a trick. So we could get that horrible, stinky cat.'

'What are you talking about?' Billy felt his grip on the doll tighten.

'After we saw you on the TV, that Colonel telephoned. He wanted to buy your disgusting cat. Mummy knew you wouldn't want to sell it, so we had to trick you.'

She put down her hairbrush and turned to face Billy. 'And you thought you could keep it. It was so funny.'

Mindy wasn't finished yet. 'And Mummy took your money too. She came in last night when you were sleeping. I saw her. She said we needed a new car, which I think is brilliant, cos ours is sooo embarrassing.'

Billy felt the room spinning. He dropped Harmony Happity Hapkins. 'I love you, Mummy. Give me a cuddle,' droned the doll as it landed on the carpet.

Billy ran from their bedroom, down the stairs and into the garden. He needed some fresh air, to clear his head. Just then he saw Phillipa Slipper walking backwards out of the shed, holding a broom at arm's length. Dangling on the end of the broom was one of the blankets Billy had wrapped around Jumblecat only last night. With her nose in the air, as if she was carrying the most disgusting thing in the world, she marched across the garden and dropped the blanket onto a bonfire, where some cushions were already smouldering away. She prodded the fire with the end of the broom, making sure nothing escaped the flames. Thick black smoke wafted up around her. She looked like a witch conjuring up a terrible spell.

So it was true. Jumblecat was gone. Billy didn't
know what to do. He felt paralysed, rooted to the
spot, but at the same time he wanted to run far
away, over Tumbledown Hill, all the way to the
sea, where he would stow away on a boat. Yes,
that was it, he would become a pirate, and sail the
seven seas and look for treasure and never have to
see his family ever again.

Just then Phillipa Slipper saw him and do you
know what she did? She laughed.

'Oh, Billy! Look at your miserable face! I wish I
had a camera. Priceless!'

*And he would become the most frightening
pirate in the world and get a parrot that pecked
out the eyes of his enemies.*

Phillipa Slipper put down the broom and walked towards him. 'You just missed the Colonel. What a lovely man. Charming. Utterly charming.'

And they would call him Captain No-Beard and his ship would be called the Jumblecat Revenge.

'Generous too! He gave me a good price for your cat. I would have accepted half what he gave me for that filthy flea bag.'

She stopped directly in front of him and bent down to within an inch of his face. 'But the good news is you're not grounded any more.'

She thought this was hilarious and laughed like a mad queen in the movies.

Not he, nor his crew of bloodthirsty pirates, would rest until Jumblecat was rescued.

CHAPTER 16

CASTLES OF ENGLAND

Billy's crew of bloodthirsty pirates was in the kitchen making tea.

'We must get him back,' insisted Mrs Mandiddee as she poured boiling water into the teapot with eight spouts. 'Straight away!'

It's true, you could hardly call Mrs Mandiddee bloodthirsty, nor was she much like a pirate (although there was the time she wore an eyepatch when she contracted conjunctivitis) but she was the best crew Billy could have wished for. She opened a new pack of Bourbons, put them on the tray with the tea and carried it through to the living room. As usual, most of the tea spilt onto the tray.

'Thank you,' he said, taking his half-empty cup.

'What we need is a plan.'

'A plan,' agreed Billy.

They sat and thought.

'Any ideas?' asked Mrs Mandiddee.

'Not yet.'

'How about a biscuit?' suggested Mrs Mandiddee, passing the plate to Billy.

They sat and thought and munched.

Billy wasn't much of a thinker. The trouble was, he muddled thinking with daydreaming. Whenever he tried to think about a serious subject, it always turned into something rather peculiar. For example, so far his plan to rescue Jumblecat involved a flying carpet and the Indian rope trick. The magic carpet would take them to Colonel Beauvrille's castle (because in Billy's mind Colonel Beauvrille was bound to live in a castle), they would lower the Indian rope, shimmy down, rescue Jumblecat, shimmy up and fly away. Easy.

Billy looked over at Mrs Mandiddee. Either she'd fallen asleep or she was putting together a brilliant plan with her eyes closed. He let his own head fall back against the sofa. By now, thick shafts of afternoon sun beamed through the window. Thousands of tiny dust particles floated lazily around the room, drifting in and out of the sunbeams. Billy focused on one dust particle as it bobbed and waltzed up past the sniffing stick, towards the top of the bookshelf. On the very top shelf it landed on a small glass bell decorated with miniature red flowers. It was a beautiful thing that Billy had never noticed before. Sunlight flooded through the bell, casting red and green shadows onto a large book. Billy cocked his head to one side and read the words running up the spine of the book. *CASTLES OF ENGLAND*.

His heart skipped a beat. If Colonel Beauvrille really did live in a castle then perhaps he would find it in this book. It was a long shot, but the way things were going, it was his only shot. So he climbed onto a chair and reached up to the top shelf.

The book was big and heavy and very, very dusty. He blew on it, sending millions more dust particles spiralling into the air. On the cover was a picture of a magnificent castle sitting proudly on top of a hill. It had a rampart and mullions and a very grand portcullis, all parts of castles that he had recently learnt at school. He mouthed the words out loud – 'Rampart, mullion, portcullis.' – words so ancient and peculiar it was as if they belonged to another language. Quietly, so as not to wake Mrs Mandiddee, he opened the book on the floor and began his search.

His eyes were getting tired and fuzzy. He had no idea there were *so* many castles in England. Tall castles, small castles, ruined castles, ugly castles, fairytale castles; but nothing about Colonel Beauvrille. Not a jot. Of course there wasn't. Why should there be? After all, the only reason he was looking through this book was because of his silly daydream. As Billy kept turning page after page he began to feel very foolish. Flying carpets! Ridiculous! He should be doing something useful to get Jumblecat back. Indian rope tricks! What a waste of time! He promised himself that from this moment on he would never daydream again. Never. Not ever.

He climbed back onto the chair with the book. It was difficult trying to squeeze *Castles of England* back into its old place. The other books, grateful for the extra space, had spread out like fat men loosening their belts after dinner. Billy stood on tiptoes, pushing with his fingertips, nearly there, just a little more . . . but it was no good. *Castles of England* slipped through his fingers and fell, pages flapping, to the floor.

Sometimes things happen for which there is no explanation. Some call this magic. Others, usually grown-ups, rant and rave until they're blue in the face that there is no such thing as magic and everything can be explained if only you look at the facts. Here are the facts. You decide.

1. *Castles of England* landed with a dull thud onto Mrs Mandiddee's carpet.

2. It landed open on page two hundred and eighty-six.

3. On page two hundred and eighty-six was a picture of a castle called Deadham Castle.

'What's so magic about that?' say the grown-ups. 'It's a book about castles. There's bound to be a castle on every page.'

Grown-ups can be very impatient.

Even before Billy had got down from the chair, he noticed there was something unusual about the picture of Deadham Castle. It wasn't the monstrous, grey tower that flanked the entrance that was unusual; nor was it the dark clouds that hovered ominously over the castle as if they were about to swallow it whole. No, there was something else. Billy got to his knees and took a closer look. Standing on the bridge that spanned the moat, was a man; a giant man with a black, bushy beard. He looked remarkably like a young Colonel Beauvrille. Billy felt a flutter of excitement. It couldn't be him, could it? Surrounding this man were a number of smaller creatures. There was a dog sitting proudly at his master's heels and there was a swan with its wings spread out wide and there was a . . . Billy rubbed his eyes, it couldn't be . . . a kangaroo! A kangaroo? Living in a castle in England? It was all too strange.

And then, Billy read the caption beneath the photo.

Colonel Charles Beauvrille, a keen taxidermist, outside Deadham Castle with a selection of his finest work.

Billy yelped with joy. It was him. He had found him, all because of his daydream and a little bit of magic.

'Magic!' scoff the grown-ups. 'Of course it wasn't

magic. It was luck that the book landed open on page two hundred and eighty-six, that's all.'

Grown-ups never learn, do they?

'What's going on?' asked Mrs Mandiddee sleepily, opening her eyes.

Billy sat next to her on the sofa with the book.

'Look what I've found,' he said, smiling broadly.

'You look like the cat that got the cream. Tell me from the beginning.'

So Billy told her about his daydream, the dust particle and the small glass bell decorated with miniature red flowers. And he told her what happened when he dropped the book.

'And it was open on this page?' asked Mrs Mandiddce.

'This very page.'

'Magic,' she said. 'I love it when magic happens.'

Some grown-ups never forget.

She took the book onto her lap. 'It certainly looks like Colonel Beauvrille.'

'But it is him. It says here.' Billy showed her the caption beneath the photo. 'What's a taxidermist, by the way?'

Instantly, the colour drained from Mrs Mandiddee's face.

'What's wrong?' asked Billy. He'd never seen her look so worried.

'Jumblecat's in trouble,' whispered Mrs Mandiddee. 'We need to get to Deadham Castle. Now.'

CHAPTER 17

A BRILLIANT PLAN

'Act normal, as if you haven't a care in the world.'

Mrs Mandiddee's advice rang round Billy's head as he opened his front door and scrunched his way up the hallway. He could hear his mother and his sister talking in the kitchen.

'Is that you, Billy?'

Billy strolled in as if nothing had happened, as if Jumblecat had never existed. Mindy was sitting at the kitchen table, brushing Harmony Happity Hapkins's hair. Phillipa Slipper stood behind Mindy, brushing her hair.

'I bet you've been with that dirty old bag lady next door,' scoffed Phillipa Slipper.

She put down the brush and made a ponytail on

top of Mindy's head. It looked like a tiny spurting hair-fountain.

'You're sick. You've definitely got Mandiddeeitus,' added Mindy, smirking. *And* she was still wearing his sash.

Billy was as cool as a cucumber. He pointed at the sash. 'It looks good on you, Mindy. You can keep it.'

'It's mine anyhow. Mummy said, didn't you.'

Phillipa Slipper nodded in agreement. 'A boy in a sash? People would laugh at you. I'm only looking after your best interests, Billy.'

'You're right,' said Billy sweetly. 'Thank you.' Inside, his blood was boiling but he had to stay calm, especially if he was to achieve his mission.

BILLY'S MISSION: GET THE CAR KEYS.

Billy put the first part of the plan into action; the brilliant plan he had devised with Mrs Mandiddee.

BILLY AND MRS MANDIDDEE'S
BRILLIANT PLAN.
PART ONE: LOOK BORED.

So he did. He looked bored. He sat down on the floor next to the fridge and thought about the most boring things in the world: table mats, broccoli, barometers, that sort of thing. He even sighed noisily to show just how bored he was.

It was the sigh that got to Mindy. 'Muuuum. Billy's annoying me. I can't concentrate on Harmony Happity Hapkins's hair.'

'I'm not doing anything,' said Billy, yawning.

She slammed her doll onto the table. 'I love you, Mummy,' it squeaked.

'Now Harmony's upset. S'not fair,' whined Mindy.

Phillipa Slipper was losing her patience. Accidently

she pulled too hard on Mindy's ponytail.

'Owww! Muuuum!'

That was it. Phillipa Slipper was annoyed.

'What's wrong with you, Billy Slipper? Haven't you got anything better to do than annoy your sister?'

The plan was going perfectly. Billy just sat there.

'Say something! Ugh! Sometimes you're just like your father. Useless. If you're so bored, why don't you go clean your room? It's a pigsty up there.'

Mindy joined in. 'And it smells. Why do I have to share a room with him? When can I have my own room, Mummy? Billy can sleep in the cellar.'

Phillipa Slipper nodded in agreement. 'You know what, Mindy, that's not a bad idea.'

It was time. Before the 'Billy-Should-Sleep-In-The-Cellar' idea went too far, he put Part Two of the brilliant plan into action.

BILLY AND MRS MANDIDDEE'S BRILLIANT PLAN.
PART TWO: OFFER TO CLEAN THE CAR.

'I could clean the car,' he said nonchalantly. 'If we're going to sell it soon, it'll need to be really clean.'

Would she fall for it? Please fall for it!

'It appears the boy has a brain after all.' Phillipa Slipper rummaged through her handbag, pulled out the car key and threw it at Billy. 'Do the inside as well.'

'It'll be good as new,' said Billy, picking up the key.

She'd fallen for it, hook, line and sinker!

'And don't think you'll be getting any pocket money for this,' yelled his mother as he walked out of the kitchen. 'I'm not made of money.'

With his back turned, she couldn't see the enormous grin on her son's face. It's a great feeling when something goes to plan. Almost as good as toffee ice cream on a sunny day. Almost.

CHAPTER 18

SPLATTAMATATTA

At Deadham Castle, Jumblecat was settling in nicely. As far as he was concerned the days of broken biscuits and draughty sheds were well behind him. And good riddance! No more tins of cat food that smelt like mouse sick. No more journeys by bus, squashed inside a manky old suitcase. From now on, it was all about fine food and luxury cars and grand old castles. At last he was being treated with the respect he deserved; after all, he was the winner of the World Fair of Curious Creatures and Strange Animals. A pedigree cat. Unique. A champion.

It had crossed his mind to ask why Colonel Beauvrille had brought him to Deadham Castle, but quite frankly, he couldn't care less, just as long as these plates of delicious food kept coming his way.

'Get me more of that pink stuff,' he demanded.

Colonel Beauvrille's patience was wearing very thin. 'The salmon's all gone,' he replied through gritted teeth. 'You finished that at lunch.'

'I'm not talking about the salmon. I know what salmon is, I'm not stupid. I want the other pink stuff, the one you gave me earlier. The fluffy stuff. What d'you call it? Taramafatter? Splattamatatta?'

'Taramasalata,' corrected Colonel Beauvrille. 'It's called taramasalata. It's a Greek delicacy made from –'

'Whatever. Just bring me buckets of it. I love it! And a bowl of milk while you're up. And a straw.'

Colonel Beauvrille had never experienced anything like this before. *He* was the one who made the rules. *He* was the one who told people what to do. Yet here he was, waiting hand and foot on a rude, jumbled-up cat.

He put the milk and taramasalata on the table. 'You forgot the straw,' said Jumblecat witheringly.

Colonel Beauvrille felt his body go tense. A peculiar throbbing filled his head as if his brain was being fish-slapped by angry monkeys. They'd spent less than a day together and already Jumblecat was pushing him towards breaking point.

But the day hadn't started like this. In fact this morning, things had been very different . . .

Phillipa Slipper screwed up her nose. 'The creature's in there,' she said, pointing at her shed. 'And please, call me Phillipa.'

'Thank you, *Phillipa*,' obliged Colonel Beauvrille. He took a large bundle of cash out of his pocket and gave it to her. 'Is this enough? A fair price for the cat? Do you think?'

Phillipa Slipper practically fainted. It was as much as the prize money she'd stolen from under her son's bed, if not more. 'Oh yes, thank you, Colonel Beauvrille.'

'Call me Charles,' he said, taking her hand and kissing it.

Phillipa Slipper quivered. No one had ever kissed her hand before. Who would dare! Of course, she'd have to wash it as soon as was decently possible. He might be a colonel and a Very Rich Man, but a beard's a beard and stink bugs lurk everywhere.

Colonel Beauvrille stepped past the curtseying Phillipa Slipper and across the garden to the shed. His beard bristled with anticipation (either that or the stink bugs were up early doing their morning exercises); this was the moment he'd been waiting for. He took a deep breath and opened the door.

There's nothing quite like getting your hands on something new for the first time, holding it, owning it, all the while thinking, *It's mine, Mine, MINE!* Whether it be a brand-new bike or an unopened packet of crisps, a chemical floods into your brain, making you feel intensely happy. And so it was with Colonel Beauvrille. He stooped down and scooped up the sleeping cat, gently cradling it in his giant arms. It was as if he was holding a newborn baby; his very own furry, feline baby.

But all that was this morning. Hours ago. Before Jumblecat had woken. Things were very different now . . .

'More steak!' ordered Jumblecat. 'And make sure you cook it properly this time. That last one was so burnt I should have called the fire brigade.' And he shoved his face so deep into the taramasalata that all you could see were the tips of his ears sticking out, like a pair of pointy periscopes.

Colonel Beauvrille wanted nothing more than to throttle this insolent, greedy, demanding, rude, overweight, jumbled-up bucket of fluff. He watched with disgust as Jumblecat came up for air, his head and whiskers encrusted in pink fluffy taramasalata, spluttering, 'Absolutely delicious,' before plunging back down for yet another face full. Usually he liked to spend a day or two with his new subjects, to get to know them a little before he began his work, but this time, with this creature, he'd already had quite enough.

'We'll be going downstairs now,' he announced suddenly. And he stood up, casting his enormous shadow over the gluttonous puss.

'What's downstairs?' asked Jumblecat.

'Oh, you'll like it down there,' lied Colonel Beauvrille. 'You can meet the others.'

'Well, as long as I don't have to share a toilet. I am special.'

Colonel Beauvrille closed his eyes and took in a deep breath. 'Oh yes. How could I forget. You are very special indeed.'

With his enormous sausage fingers he picked up Jumblecat by the scruff of his neck and held him at arm's length, careful not to splatter taramasalata on his tweed suit.

'But I haven't finished my splattamatatta yet,' whinged the dangling cat.

'Diddums,' replied the Colonel, and headed downstairs.

CHAPTER 19

IT'S LIKE RIDING A BICYCLE

Mrs Mandiddee hadn't driven for thirty years. 'What does this thing do?' she asked, pulling on a lever.

With a grinding crunch the car lurched forward.

'Hee hee. This is fun. Oh, hang on, I remember.'

She pushed her foot down on the accelerator. REVVVVVVVUM. The car made a lot of noise, but didn't budge.

'Don't you need to take the handbrake off?' suggested Billy, buckling up his seatbelt.

'Silly me!'

Billy was getting nervous. They were still in the drive. Phillipa Slipper was bound to hear something.

'I thought you said you can drive,' said Billy.

'It's like riding a bicycle, my dear, once you learn you never forget.'

And suddenly they were off, moving onto the street like a jumpy snail. Billy looked over his shoulder, fully expecting to see his mother chasing after them with a hairbrush.

'Is it stealing if the owner gives you the key?' asked Billy.

'We've only borrowed it. She'll get her precious car back as soon as we get Jumblecat back.'

'I know, but –'

'Now stop worrying and find a map. I haven't got a clue where I'm going.'

Billy did as he was told and opened the glove compartment. He pulled out a map so old and tattered it looked like it had been to the moon and back. The car lurched forward again.

'Sorry,' giggled Mrs Mandiddee. 'Wrong pedal.'

As Billy opened the map, something fell out onto his lap. It was a black-and-white photograph of a young man and a dog in a snow-covered field. The man wore a woolly bobble hat and was smiling straight into the camera. The dog had a snowball in its mouth and was leaping up at the man. It took a moment for Billy to recognise the man as his dad, not because he was so young, but because he was smiling. Billy had never seen his dad smile. Yet here he was, grinning from ear to ear, happy as can be.

And then the strangest thing happened. As Billy slipped the photograph into his pocket, he looked out of the window and at that very moment, that split second, he saw his dad, standing beside his milk float, staring right back at him. Their eyes locked.

'Did you see that?' Billy yelped as the car screeched around a corner.

'See what?' replied Mrs Mandiddee. 'Oh, fishcakes! It wasn't a policeman, was it?'

'No. I think I saw my . . .'

Billy stopped. It had all happened so quickly perhaps he had imagined the whole thing. It wouldn't be the first time his imagination had played tricks on him. But it seemed so real, right down to the very surprised expression on his dad's face.

By the time they got out of town, Mrs Mandiddee had gone through two red traffic lights, narrowly missed a parked tree and screeched to a halt at a

zebra crossing to allow a pigeon to cross the road. And now it was getting late. Long, dark shadows crept across the country lanes and, according to the map, Deadham Castle was still some way away. It would be almost dark by the time they got there.

'We could just knock on Colonel Beauvrille's door,' suggested Billy. 'I'll tell him there's been a terrible mix-up and Jumblecat was never for sale in the first place.'

'I don't think that's such a good idea,' replied Mrs Mandiddee.

'But why? I'm sure he'd understand.'

'Billy, I don't think Colonel Beauvrille wants to keep Jumblecat as a pet.'

'Why else would he want him?'

Mrs Mandiddee took a deep breath. 'You remember you asked me what taxidermist means?'

Billy nodded. Somehow he could tell he wasn't going to like this.

'A taxidermist is someone who stuffs dead animals. Colonel Beauvrille likes stuffing animals. All those animals in the book weren't alive, they were stuffed.'

Billy remembered the picture of the young Colonel Beauvrille surrounded by the dog, the swan with the outstretched wings and the kangaroo. They seemed so real. Well, they were real, but just not very alive.

'You really think Colonel Beauvrille wants to stuff Jumblecat?' he said eventually.

'Yes, dear, I do.'

'But how can he stuff Jumblecat if he's not dead?'

But as soon as he'd asked the question, he knew the answer. Colonel Beauvrille wasn't interested in living creatures at all. Billy tried to imagine his jumbled-up four-legged friend stuffed full of old newspaper or tummy button fluff, or whatever taxidermists used. He wouldn't let it happen. They had to get to the castle as quickly as possible.

'Does this car go any faster?' asked Billy.

'I don't think so, but I'll try.'

She pushed her foot right down on the accelerator. The car heaved and groaned and somehow picked up speed.

Mrs Mandiddee let out a squeal of excitement. 'Whaaahoooo! Not bad for an old girl.'

Billy wasn't sure if she was talking about the car or her driving. Either way, they were really motoring now. He gripped the sides of his seat and gritted his teeth.

'We're coming, Jumblecat,' he said under his breath. 'We're coming.'

CHAPTER 20

USELESS MAN

Phillipa Slipper had made up her mind. It was all Christopher Slipper's fault.

'The boy's a delinquent. If you were any kind of father then none of this would have happened,' she said, dragging a bag full of stuff down the stairs.

'Never would have happened,' chimed Mindy from the top of the stairs.

Christopher Slipper had just got home from his milk round. He stepped into the hallway and took off his shoes.

'He's only gone and stolen the car,' said Phillipa Slipper. 'I bet he's gone to find that hideous cat I sold to Colonel Beauvrille.' She glared at her husband. 'Did you hear me? Your son has stolen the car.'

Christopher Slipper looked at the bag she was dragging down the stairs. It was full of Billy's Collectabillya. A piece of bark in the shape of a star fell out and slid down the stairs in front of her. She stamped on it, splitting it in two.

'Useless junk. I should never have allowed him to bring it into the house in the first place. Well, don't just stand there. Pick it up.'

As usual, Christopher Slipper did as he was told.

'If he behaves like a rat, then he can live like a rat. From now on Billy Slipper lives in the cellar.' She opened the cellar door and threw the bag down the stairs.

'And I get the whole bedroom to myself,' added Mindy joyfully, doing a little dance that made her look like she needed to go to the toilet.

Christopher Slipper scrunched into the kitchen and opened the fridge door. He always had a large glass of milk when he finished work.

'Oh no you don't,' snarled Phillipa Slipper, slamming the fridge door shut. 'There's work to be done. His mattress needs to be brought down and the whole room needs a good hoovering. You can't expect Mindy to sleep in there like that. She'll catch a disease. You've already ruined one of my children. I'll not have you mess the other one up.'

Mindy came into the kitchen carrying three ugly dolls with horribly singed hair. From now on they could live in the cellar with Billy.

'Who's got a disease?' she asked.

'I think your father's got a disease,' smirked Phillipa Slipper. 'He's got the useless disease.' She thought this was terribly funny and did her mad queen laugh. Mindy joined in, cackling like a mad princess, though she didn't really understand what she was laughing about.

Phillipa Slipper wasn't finished yet. 'Look. He can't speak either. Maybe that disgusting cat got his tongue.'

'Cat got your tongue,' echoed Mindy, sticking out her tongue at her dad.

Christopher Slipper scrunched out of the kitchen and up the stairs. Halfway up he stopped, listening to his wife and daughter make fun of him. He stood there for some time. Just listening. Then, unexpectedly, he turned, went back downstairs and walked straight out of the house. He didn't even put his shoes on. He jumped into his milk float and drove away in his socks. Of course, nobody even noticed he'd gone.

CHAPTER 21

SING FOR ME

Jumblecat crash-landed onto a hard, metal table.

'Owwww!' he miaow-moaned. 'You didn't have to drop me.'

'Oh, I'm sorry,' said Colonel Beauvrille, sounding none too sorry. 'Butterfingers.'

He opened a drawer on the side of the table, took out a small, clear bottle and gave it a vigorous shake.

Jumblecat looked around. Above him, rows of powerful strip lights hung from the ceiling. It was incredibly, blindingly bright. 'What is this place?' he asked. 'Am I going to be sleeping down here?'

'You could say that,' replied Colonel Beauvrille enigmatically. He held the bottle up to the light and read the tiny print on the label.

'Well, you'll have to turn these lights down. I can't sleep if there's too much light. Where's my bed?'

'Oh, take your pick.' Colonel Beauvrille gestured around the room. 'There's plenty to choose from.'

Jumblecat arched his head back against the stainless-steel table. As far as he could make out, there were no beds or sofas or anything soft for sleeping on. The floor was white and hard and cold. Around the edge of the room he could see lots of metal bars, boxed, like prison windows. Jumblecat squinted, trying to block out some of the harsh light. Lurking in the darkness behind the bars were strange shadows, indistinguishable and motionless like fuzzy statues.

'Who are they?' asked Jumblecat.

'It's only the others. Don't worry about them. Rest assured, they won't disturb you. I'm sure you'll find your . . . *accommodation* very comfortable. Perhaps sir will be requiring room service? Breakfast at eight?' Colonel Beauvrille could barely suppress his sniggers. 'You'll find a shower cap and complimentary soap in the en suite bathroom. I do hope you have a pleasant stay here at Deadham Castle Hotel.' And he burst into one of his curiously high-pitched giggles that echoed shrilly around the room.

Now he was enjoying himself. With a dramatic flourish, he whipped out a syringe from the top drawer and thrust the needle through the lid of the small, clear bottle. Steadily, he pulled back the plunger and filled the glass barrel with liquid. 'It won't hurt. In fact, quite the opposite. It'll help you relax.'

Things were taking an unexpectedly unpleasant turn. 'I'm very relaxed already,' insisted Jumblecat, anxiously eyeing up the syringe. 'Look how relaxed I am.' To prove it, he flopped his legs and tail down onto the metal table. 'See! I'm RELAXED!'

Colonel Beauvrille leant down close to Jumblecat's face. Too close. Jumblecat could see every wiry hair that sprouted out of Colonel Beauvrille's nose and his breath smelt like unkind mushrooms.

'Don't be scared. I'm going to make you famous. Forever.' Colonel Beauvrille pinched the scruff of Jumblecat's neck. A fat fold of fur bulged out. 'Don't move,' he said, as he slowly moved the needle towards Jumblecat's neck.

'Wait! What are you doing? I'll be good!'

Something snapped in Colonel Beauvrille. 'Good?' he hollered. 'Goooooood? You haven't been *good* from the moment you set foot in my castle. You have been rude, impertinent, astronomically greedy, demanding, impolite, disrespectful, ill-mannered, bad-mannered, foul-mannered and loutish; but not once have you been good.'

All of a sudden he stood bolt upright, closed his eyes and inhaled deeply, three times.

Eventually, a calmer Colonel Beauvrille opened his eyes and stared sadly at Jumblecat. 'Sing for me. One last time.'

'What?' guffawed Jumblecat incredulously. 'I can't sing.'

'Sing for me,' repeated Colonel Beauvrille. 'Like you did at the competition. Sing for me. Make me cry.'

The man was bonkers.

'Don't be shy. When you sing I feel like I'm drowning in the sweetest honey.'

This must be some kind of joke, thought Jumblecat. *Drowning in honey? Any minute now that Slipper boy and that scrawny old Mandiddee woman are going to charge in yelling, 'Fooled you!' and everyone will have a good old laugh.*

'SING!' roared Colonel Beauvrille, waving the needle menacingly close to Jumblecat's neck once again.

Obediently, Jumblecat began singing.

Do you remember how beautifully Jumblecat sang in the Old Grand Hall? How he seduced the audience with his melodious miaows, reducing Colonel Beauvrille to tears? Well, that was when he was asleep. When he was awake, he was ear-bleedingly awful. He hacked and croaked and spat out noises that were as far from singing as we are from the moon. A saw cutting through rusty metal would have been more musical. Wizened fingernails scraping down a blackboard would have been more harmonious. A sunburnt frog would have been more tuneful.

Colonel Beauvrille clamped his hands over his ears. 'Enough,' he wailed. 'Stop!'

But Jumblecat was beginning to enjoy himself. 'I'm singing,' he told himself. 'Listen to me, I'm singing! And people say that cat's can't sing. Nonsense! Tommyrot! I can SING!'

Jumblecat never felt the needle sink into his neck. His terrible song still echoed around the room as he slumped silently across the stainless-steel table.

CHAPTER 22

DEADHAM CASTLE

Billy and Mrs Mandiddee got out of the car. Ahead of them the road sloped down into a wide, open valley. The evening sun was drifting behind the hills, bathing the countryside in a sleepy, orange glow. And there, on the far side of the valley, was Deadham Castle. It rose out of the ground like a stone fist, strong and fierce. It was nearly five hundred years old but looked as dark and powerful as the day it was built.

'Can you see it?' asked Billy.

Mrs Mandiddee nodded.

'What do we do now?'

'I don't know, but we'll think of something. Come on, let's get going before it gets too dark.'

They turned to get back into the car. But the car was already halfway down the hill, rolling down the road, gliding silently away.

Billy and Mrs Mandiddee just stood there, open-mouthed, watching. There was nothing they could do.

The road curved away at the bottom. Naturally, the car went straight on, plunging through a tall hedgerow. There was no great crash or mighty explosion, just a gentle metallic burp, as the car came to rest in a ditch with the exhaust pipe sticking up into the sky. One of the back wheels spun round and round like some rickety old funfair ride.

'I think I forgot to put the handbrake on,' whispered Mrs Mandiddee. 'Sorry.'

Billy tried to imagine telling Phillipa Slipper how they destroyed her car. He imagined the sixteen shades of red her face would turn, all the way from angry cerise to blistering scarlet.

This time it was Mrs Mandiddee's turn to ask the question, 'What do we do now?'

There was nothing else for it. 'We walk,' answered Billy, striding off in the direction of Deadham Castle.

They passed the car parked upright in the ditch. It seemed very peaceful, as if it was just having an upside-down rest. A curious sheep nibbled at the wing mirror, but finding nothing of interest, went back to her evening grazing. By now the sun had slipped behind the hills. They decided not to walk along the road; it was much quicker to go as the crow flies and head directly to the castle across the fields.

Apart from the light of a not-so-new-moon, the valley slipped into darkness. There were no streetlights or car headlights, nor were there any lights coming from the castle. It seemed deserted. Billy began to worry. What if Colonel Beauvrille didn't live here any more? Had they travelled all this way in a stolen, (smashed-up) car for nothing? Jumblecat could be miles away being stuffed with newspaper and tummy button fluff while they trudged across a valley. And all because he'd found a picture in an old book.

The mighty tower of Deadham Castle loomed above them; four solid walls of stone with two narrow slits for windows. Once upon a time burning arrows would have shot out of these windows at invading armies, but tonight they were as still as a pair of dark, dead eyes.

Billy and Mrs Mandiddee came to the edge of a river and followed it upstream. Clumps of bulrushes rose like spears from the bank. Everywhere Billy looked, he saw strange shapes and shadows hanging in the darkness. He decided to concentrate on Mrs Mandiddee's feet ahead of him, left foot, right foot, left foot, right foot, moving lightly through the grass. She had a small hole in the back of her left sock, just big enough to fit a pea. Squeeze in enough peas and she could make mushy peas as she walked. Somehow the thought of mushy peas made him feel less anxious. Just follow the feet, left foot, right foot, left foot . . .

'Look!' whispered Mrs Mandiddee, stopping suddenly.

It was just as it was in the book; a long wooden bridge that sloped gently up and over the river and into the castle.

'What's the plan?' asked Billy. He was sure Mrs Mandiddee would have a plan.

Her gap-toothed smile glistened in the light of the not-so-new-moon. 'I was going to ask you the same thing.'

Planless, they crossed the bridge and passed under a fearsome-looking portcullis. The row of steel teeth hovering above looked sharp enough to crush an elephant, let alone a boy. Billy decided there and then never to linger under a portcullis again, just in case.

Beyond the portcullis was a large, gravelled courtyard and there, parked in the middle, was a black Rolls-Royce.

'That's it!' Billy whispered excitedly. 'That's the car I saw this morning. It's Colonel Beauvrille's car.' They had come to the right place after all.

'Now all we've got to do is find Jumblecat and take him home,' said Mrs Mandiddee. She made it sound so easy.

Billy counted twelve doors dotted around the courtyard. They were all identical; heavy, wooden doors fortified with black metal studs, each with a keyhole large enough to fit a frozen fish finger.

'Which one?' whispered Billy.

'You decide.'

Billy's lucky number was seven. Ever since he had found seven four-leaf clovers growing together in the field behind his house, he'd always believed – well, half believed – that seven brought him luck. Also his birthday was on the seventh, so that must mean something, probably. He counted from the left. Door seven was almost directly in front of them, on the far side of the courtyard.

'Are you ready?' asked Mrs Mandiddee. Her eyes were twinkling with excitement.

Billy nodded. 'On three.'

On the count of three, they stepped out of the shadows.

CHAPTER 23

THE TAXIDERMIST'S TEA PARTY

SCRUNCH! Have you ever tried to walk on gravel really quietly? SCRUNCH SCRUNCH! It's impossible. In fact, according to world experts and scientists, gravel is the fourth noisiest thing you can walk on.

(Incidentally, the top five noisiest things to walk on are:

Snails

Twigs

Drawing pins – especially if you're not wearing shoes

Gravel

Bubble wrap.)

SCRUNCH SCRUNCH SCRUNCH! Their

footsteps echoed all around the castle walls. They tried treading on tiptoes, but it made no difference. Billy was convinced an enraged colonel would at any moment burst out in his pyjamas, wielding a shotgun. But no one came, nor did any lights come on in the castle windows.

'Go on, open it,' urged Mrs Mandiddee when they reached the seventh door.

He pushed down the handle but it was locked. So much for lucky number seven. Doors eight, nine and ten were all locked as well, but door eleven swung open. Eleven was definitely his new lucky number.

It was gloomy inside. 'Can you see anything?' asked Billy in such a quiet whisper that he barely heard himself.

'Not a thing,' replied Mrs Mandiddee. 'There must be a light switch somewhere.' She felt around the walls. 'I think I've found something. Shall I try it?'

Even before Mrs Mandiddee switched on the light Billy had already decided what he was going to see. Everyone knows what the inside of a castle looks like. There'd be heraldic shields and an enormous, fading tapestry depicting a battle or a hunting scene. Then there'd be paintings of serious-looking ancestors and, of course, a suit of armour standing guard holding one of those ball and chain things that knights used to smash their way through enemy lines. Billy had seen it all a thousand times before . . .

Mrs Mandiddee turned on the lights.

Gathered around a dining-room table were fifteen stuffed animals having the most elegant, extravagant, extraordinary tea party. At the head of the table sat a pig, dressed in a pinstripe suit. In one trotter he held an enormous cigar, while the other reached across the table towards a pile of cucumber sandwiches. Next to him sat a chicken, propped up on two cushions so it could reach the table. Strapped to its head was a tall bonnet decorated with tiny bells that no doubt would make a delightful ring if she ever moved her feathered head. But that wasn't going to happen anytime soon.

'It's a taxidermist's tea party,' said Mrs Mandiddee wandering around the table. 'A never-ending feast. Look! An octopus!'

Its tentacles spread in every direction. One was wrapped around a cream cake, another around a biscuit and a third hovered over two plates, as if it was unable to decide between the lemon tart and the meringues. The fourth tentacle held a piece of

toast and the fifth buttered it with a silver knife. The sixth tentacle went somewhere under the table, the seventh held a pork pie tantalisingly in front of its mouth and the last one rested tenderly on the arm of a mustachioed monkey sitting two places away.

The largest creature around the table was a horse. Somehow it had squeezed its hind legs under the table while its front legs reared up into the air as if it had just heard the funniest thing. Around its ears it wore a garland of flowers and it appeared to be wearing lipstick.

At the other end of the table, opposite the pig, were two empty chairs.

'Do you think Colonel Beauvrille and his wife sit there?' Billy asked.

'Maybe,' replied Mrs Mandiddee. 'Is he married?'

'I don't know. Maybe he saves it for a special guest.' Just then, Billy had a terrible thought. 'Mrs M., do you think it might be Jumblecat's place?'

But before she could answer, a piercing cry came from somewhere deep in the castle.

Billy and Mrs Mandiddee froze. For a moment they were as still as the animals around the table, as if they themselves were part of the taxidermist's tea party.

There it was again; a distant wailing, like a baby's cry or an animal in distress. The hairs on the back of Billy's neck stood to attention. Jumblecat!

At the far end of the dining room was a wooden door. They had both been too preoccupied by the tea party to even notice it before. Billy put his ear next to the keyhole and listened.

'It was Jumblecat. I'm sure of it,' said Billy, looking up at his old friend.

Slowly Billy turned the handle and pushed open the door. He peered into the darkness. 'I can't see a thing,' he whispered.

'Wait a minute,' said Mrs Mandiddee. 'I've got an idea.'

She hurried back to the table and squeezed in between the dog and the horse.

'Excuse me,' she said politely as she stretched across the table and picked up a candlestick with three candles in it. Then she went to the head of the table and felt around in the pig's waistcoat pocket. Triumphantly she pulled out a box of matches.

'How did you know they'd be there?' Billy asked as they lit the candles.

'He's holding a cigar,' she replied. 'He had to have something to light it with.'

The taxidermist had thought of everything for the perfect party.

They entered a corridor lined with portraits of Colonel Beauvrille's ancestors. They certainly were an ugly-looking bunch.

'Look at this one,' whispered Mrs Mandiddee.

She held the candlestick up to a portrait of a man with enormous side whiskers; his screwed-up face made him look like he'd just eaten the sourest lemon imaginable. His name, according to the plaque beneath, was Sir Theodore Beauvrille. In his hand he held a surgeon's knife and draped over his shoulder was a fox pelt, with the head still attached. Billy shivered. This was not the kind of man you would want to bump into in a dark castle on a stormy night.

As they moved down the corridor, each portrait was as disagreeable as the one before. There was one man with a head like a pineapple and another with rotten teeth the colour of custard. And the women weren't much better. Even the flickering candlelight couldn't hide their ugliness. Clearly, no Beauvrille woman had ever won a beauty contest, covered as they were in facial boils and lady moustaches. Towards the end of the corridor there was a portrait of Lord Albermoulde, also known as Le Mad Lord, and who, according to the label underneath the portrait, was the first owner of Deadham Castle. In his arms he held a chicken rather bizarrely dressed in a green velvet smock. Lord Albermoulde looked cheerfully out of the picture as if to say, 'I don't care what you think of me. I'm happy.' It was the only portrait Billy liked. It reminded him how he felt about Jumblecat and how he didn't care if other people thought that was strange.

At the end of the corridor there was a spiral staircase that twisted sharply up.

'This way,' said Mrs Mandiddee, bounding up the stairs two at a time like a woman half her age, or a quarter of her age, or even an eighth of her age.

Billy followed. He watched her shadow dance and flicker on the stone walls as they climbed the tower. Up and up they went. Around every corner Billy expected to reach the top, but there were just more stairs.

'MIIIIAAAAOOOOWWWW.'

They were getting close. Jumblecat was close. It was almost as if he was guiding them to him.

At last, after one hundred and twenty-seven steps (Billy always counted steps), they reached the top. He sat down to catch his breath. Out of a slit window he could see the not-so-new-moon hovering in the night sky. Mrs Mandiddee put the candlestick down and rested with him.

'Are you OK?' she asked in between breaths.

Billy nodded. 'You?'

'Piece of cake,' she puffed, smiling back at him. 'Which way now?'

Just then Billy felt something crawl over the back of his hand. A small spider scuttled down his little finger and back onto the floor. He liked spiders, even the big ones, and would always rescue them if they got stuck in the bath. Once, he spent an afternoon constructing an escape ladder out of string and matchsticks and draped it over the side of the bath. That way they could always get out if they ever fell in. Of course, Mindy had sneered at his efforts and told Phillipa Slipper. 'Just drown them,' his mother had snapped as she broke the ladder into tiny pieces. 'It's much simpler. Turn on the tap and sluice them down the plughole.' He imagined that one day the spiders would return his act of kindness. Perhaps this was that moment.

The spider hesitated a moment, then scuttled under a door.

'Jumblecat's in there,' Billy whispered. 'I'm sure of it.' He lay down on his tummy and peeked under the door. A faint, flickering light came from inside the room.

'What can you see?' asked Mrs Mandiddee.

'I'm not sure,' he replied, squashing his face even closer to the door. 'Maybe it's nothing but . . .'

'MIIIIAAAAOOOOWWWW.'

Billy leapt to his feet and without hesitation flung open the door.

CHAPTER 24

A CAT IN A DOG

'Come in,' said Colonel Beauvrille calmly. 'Both of you. Come in.' It was as if he had been expecting them all along.

He was sitting in an armchair next to a roaring fire. Curled up on his lap a Chihuahua was sleeping peacefully. Colonel Beauvrille reached over and pulled a long, metal fork out of the flames. On the end was a lightly toasted marshmallow.

'I know it's extravagant lighting a fire on a warm summer's evening, but I just love toasted marshmallows.' Curiously, he pronounced marshmallows like 'marshmelloze'. 'The funny thing is,' he continued, 'marshmelloze taste vile unless they're toasted. Too chewy. Like eating a rubber band, don't you think?' Billy wasn't sure if he was supposed to answer or not.

Colonel Beauvrille held the fork at arm's length and put the marshmallow in his mouth, sucking off just the outer layer. Then he put the fork back in the fire and began toasting the gooey inside.

'One layer at a time. It's the best way, don't you think?'

Billy couldn't keep quiet any longer. 'Where is he? Where's Jumblecat?' He felt his cheeks going bright red.

'Oh yes, Jumblecat,' said Colonel Beauvrille, licking marshmallow off his lips. 'Do you know, the first time I laid eyes on Jumblecat, I said to myself, I said, "Charles, what a specimen! What a creature! I want it. I want it. I want it."' Colonel Beauvrille turned and stared sadly at Billy. 'It almost seems a shame I have to stuff him, though he is terribly rude, don't you find?'

'We know he's in here. We heard him,' insisted Mrs Mandiddee.

'You heard him did you? Perhaps you only think you heard him,' replied Colonel Beauvrille. He was clearly enjoying himself. With his giant hand, he picked up the Chihuahua from his lap. The dog didn't uncurl. In fact, it was as stiff as a board.

'Listen to this,' he said and squeezed the Chihuahua's stomach.

'MIIIIAAAAOOOOWWWW,' went the stuffed dog.

'Isn't it wonderful!' he chuckled. 'It's like a cat inside a dog.'

Like a child showing off his favourite toy, he squeezed it again.

'MIIIIAAAAOOOOWWWW.'

And again.

'MIIIIAAAAOOOOWWWW.'

And again.

'MIIIIAAAAOOOOWWWW.'

MIAOW!

And he fell into a curiously high-pitched giggling fit until tears rolled down his face. Eventually he pulled a tweed handkerchief out of his pocket and dabbed his eyes.

'Wonderful! Don't you think? Of course other taxidermists think I'm very unprofessional. "You shouldn't be doing this," they say. "Goes against our code of conduct," they say. Well, I say, "Phooey!" All they want to do is stuff the animal and put it on display. Boring! I want to *play* with my creations. I trust you enjoyed the tea party?'

Mrs Mandiddee stepped forward. 'We only want Jumblecat back. He belongs to the boy.'

With great effort, Colonel Beauvrille heaved himself out of his armchair. Billy had forgotten how enormous the man was. The top of his head almost touched the ceiling.

'I don't think you understand me,' he said, pacing the room. He seemed to be getting upset. 'When my great-grandfather, Theodore Beauvrille, captured and stuffed the last living dodo on the planet, it was *his* masterpiece. All my life I've been waiting for a moment like this. When I stuff your cat, it will be *my* masterpiece. This', he declared, waving the Chihuahua in the air, 'is nothing.' And he threw the stuffed animal onto the fire.

The Chihuahua gave one last feeble miaow before being engulfed by the flames.

Colonel Beauvrille's voice grew louder. 'Jumblecat is *mine*. I bought him fair and square from your delightful mother. Marvelleeus woman. Please give her my regards. Oh, silly me, I don't think you'll be seeing her for some time.'

'What are you talking about?' said Billy.

Colonel Beauvrille positioned himself by the door. His eyes were as wide as ping-pong balls.

'You know, I've never tried to stuff a child before. I wonder how difficult it would be?' He looked at Mrs Mandiddee. 'Though I couldn't do you. Too scrawny. Looks like you're made up of leaves and twigs as it is.'

He slammed the door behind him and locked it.

'By the way,' he bellowed through the keyhole, 'help yourselves to marshmelloze. I couldn't stand it if you thought of me as a bad host.'

He thought this was tremendously funny and giggled all the way down the stairs.

Mrs Mandiddee was furious. 'Come back here and I'll show you what leaves and twigs can do!' she bellowed, beating her fists against the door.

Billy had never seen Mrs Mandiddee so angry, but already his mind was elsewhere. On escape.

CHAPTER 25

NEVER TRUST A MARSHMALLOW

They were well and truly trapped. The walls were made of solid stone and the window was just a narrow slit. They checked for trapdoors, secret passages, anything. Billy even looked up the chimney once the fire had died down; perhaps he could crawl up it and escape over the roof. Mrs Mandiddee wasn't so keen. When she was a little girl, she remembered hearing stories about boys being sent up chimneys to clean them and never coming down.

Before too long, despite everything, Mrs Mandiddee fell asleep in the armchair. At first she refused to even sit in it. 'I'm not sitting anywhere where *that man* has parked his enormous bottom,' was her response. But seeing as it was the only comfortable seat in the room, Billy was eventually able to persuade her to use it.

'What about you, my dear?' she asked.

Even before Billy could reply, her eyes had closed. He found an old sheepskin rug, shook it for dust and laid it gently over her.

Billy sat down on the stone window seat and tried to think. He felt so tired and drained that all his thoughts were getting muddy.

Concentrate, Billy. How to escape?

He considered smoke signals, but to whom? There was no one around for miles and even if there was, who would see them at night? A carpet, rolled up in the corner of the room, caught his eye. It might just be magic. Of course it was. A magic carpet! He stumbled over and unrolled it and issued every magic command he could think of, from abracadabra to zalamoosh, but of course, it stayed firmly on the floor. Dreamily, he thought about climbing out of the window. Surely he could jump onto the not-so-new-moon and slide down the crescent onto the top of the hills? But his head was marginally too big to squeeze through the window. He imagined Mindy watching him as he tried. 'Big head,' she would call him, and big head he was.

He heard scrunching coming from outside. He peeked out of the window and watched as Colonel Beauvrille strode across the gravelled courtyard, unlocked door number seven and went in. A minute later he reappeared, holding a jar. A pink light emanated from inside the jar, lighting up the Colonel's face like a puffy blancmange. He locked the door again, put the keys in his tweed-jacket pocket and scrunched his way back across the courtyard.

The thought of blancmange made Billy's tummy rumble. Apart from a couple of biscuits that morning, he realised he hadn't eaten all day. Lying on the floor next to the fireplace was the half-empty packet of marshmallows. He wouldn't eat them; he wouldn't accept anything from Colonel Beauvrille. After all, the man had threatened to stuff him. But the marshmallows looked so good; in fact, they were one of his favourite things, toasted or not. One of the marshmallows had fallen out of the packet and lay on the marble hearth. It couldn't hurt to eat one, could it?

'Please eat me,' said the marshmallow rather sadly.

Billy rubbed his eyes. Marshmallows, particularly

pink ones, can't talk. He was overtired and hungry, that's all.

'Sleepy, are you?' asked the marshmallow. It was quite considerate.

'Yes,' said Billy. 'It's been a long day.'

'You know, you could always use us as a pillow.'

'Don't be silly,' Billy replied. 'Marshmallows are for eating, not sleeping on.'

'But we're so soft. Go on. Try it!'

'But I need to stay awake. I've got to find a way out of here.' Billy knew it was ridiculous having a conversation with a marshmallow, but it did have a point; they were very soft, just like tiny pillows.

The marshmallow didn't give up. 'Well, how about a little snooze. Just ten minutes. To clear your head.'

Now this made sense. 'OK,' he said. 'But just for ten minutes. Promise me you'll wake me up?'

'Promise,' said the marshmallow.

So Billy took out the remaining marshmallows from the packet, arranged them on the window sill and rested his head on them. They cushioned him like the softest pillow.

'Just ten minutes,' he insisted. He could feel himself drifting off already.

'Just ten minutes,' whispered the marshmallow sweetly into his ear.

Of course, marshmallows have no understanding of time. They can't count ten minutes any better than a cauliflower or a brick. In fact, marshmallows aren't much use for anything. If you needed help making your bed, you wouldn't ask a marshmallow; if the dog needed a walk, you know a marshmallow wouldn't do it for you. (The dog would probably eat it anyhow.) Likewise, if ever you're late for school, don't tell your teacher that a marshmallow forgot to wake you up. Your teacher won't believe you and you'll have to stay behind after school and write out a hundred times:

I MUST NOT USE A MARSHMALLOW AS AN ALARM CLOCK.
I MUST NOT USE A MARSHMALLOW AS AN ALARM CLOCK.
I MUST NOT USE A MARSHMALLOW AS AN ALARM CLOCK.

. . . and ninety-seven more times.

Never trust a marshmallow. Especially pink ones.

CHAPTER 26

CACOPHONOUS SNORING AND A MILKMAN

Even as a boy, Colonel Beauvrille snored very, very loudly. His parents, exhausted from a lack of sleep, moved his bed to the old vegetable cellar deep under the castle. Every evening at bedtime, young Charles, wearing his pyjamas and carrying his favourite raggedy teddy bear, crossed the gravelled courtyard and went down to his underground bedroom. It smelt down there. Three hundred years of storing cabbages and potatoes had left an indelible and pungent stink. For a while, this arrangement worked well, but as he grew bigger his snoring grew louder. The doctors said there was nothing they could do, so in desperation his parents sent him away, first to boarding school, then the Army and then to travel the world. When both his parents died unexpectedly on safari in Africa (their tent was squashed by an amorous, short-sighted hippopotamus), he moved back in to Deadham Castle.

Soon after, he married, but his new wife left him after only three days. The snoring was just too much for her to bear. He bought a dog, but it ran away. So did the cat. Then one day, while browsing in the castle library for a cure for snoring, he came across a book written by his great-grandfather, the notorious taxidermist Theodore Beauvrille. It was a revelation. If he could master the art of taxidermy then nothing would run away from him ever again. From that day on, Colonel Beauvrille stuffed anything he could lay his hands on. At first he wasn't very good at it – his squirrels ended up looking like rats and his rats ended up looking like sausages – but after much practice, he became something of an expert.

Like many before him, Billy was woken up by Colonel Beauvrille's snoring. It sounded like a low-flying aeroplane rumbling back and forth over the castle, shaking the very foundations. Now that he was awake, he realised he felt terrible; it was cold and his whole body ached from sleeping in such an awkward position. Despite the terrible noise, Mrs Mandiddee was still fast asleep in the armchair. She looked so cosy and comfortable that Billy thought about lying down and using the not-so-magic carpet as a blanket. But there was no way he'd get back to sleep, not with that cacophonous snoring. Besides, he still had to work out how they were going to get out of here.

He stood up and stretched his arms to the ceiling, uncurling his aching body. Outside, it was starting to get light and the moon was fading away like a weary ghost after a long night's haunting. And that's when he saw something. Two pinpricks of light coming over the brow of the hill, moving down into the valley. It was a vehicle of some sort with its headlights on. It moved slowly and methodically, weaving its way along the road towards the castle. As it drew closer, Billy heard something so familiar, so every day, that at first he didn't believe what his ears were telling him.

'It can't be,' he whispered to himself.

But there it was again, the faint but unmistakable sound of milk bottles clinking together in their crates.

'The milkman!' Billy said out loud. 'It's the milkman!'

Mrs Mandiddee opened her eyes. 'Oh dear me, did I fall asleep?' She heard the snoring. 'What's that terrible noise?'

Billy couldn't get his words out fast enough. 'Quick! Mrs M! There's a milkman coming. We've got to get a message to him and maybe he can pass a message on to my dad. All milkmen know each other, don't they? Aren't there milkmen clubs, where milkmen get together and talk about . . . erm . . . milk?'

'Why don't we just shout down to him when he gets here?'

'But it might wake up Colonel Beauvrille. Can't you hear his snoring?'

'I thought that was an aeroplane or a . . . what's that on your forehead?' she asked, pointing at the marshmallows glued to him.

But Billy wasn't listening. He was scurrying around the room looking for a pen and paper. Next to the door he found a pile of old books. He opened the top one and ripped out a blank page near the front. Already, he could hear the gentle whirring of the electric milk float getting closer. It reminded him of lying in bed at home, listening to his dad, going off to work. *Concentrate, Billy! No time for daydreaming!*

'A pen. A pen. Have you got a pen?' he babbled.

'No, but . . .' Mrs Mandiddee looked around the room for something they could write with. 'Quick. Give me the paper.'

She knelt in front of the fireplace and pulled out a half-burnt stick. With the charred end she scrawled on the paper:

HELD PRISONER. GET HELP.

Mrs Mandiddee's handwriting was pretty bad at the best of times. Writing with a charred stick did nothing to improve it. In fact, it looked like she'd written:

HELL POISONER. GOT HILP.

'What's hilp?' asked Billy, reading over her shoulder.

'It says help. H-e-l-p,' spelt Mrs Mandiddee helpfully.

'No it doesn't. It says . . .'

The milk float pulled into the gravelled courtyard. There was no time for rewrites. They dashed to the narrow window and watched as the milk float came to a stop next to the Rolls-Royce. Billy screwed up the piece of paper and stretched his arm out through the window.

Mrs Mandiddee stood above him. 'Careful now,' she whispered. 'Take aim. Fire.'

With a flick of the wrist, Billy threw the paper ball. It drifted down and landed, with a gentle 'plop' on the roof of the milk float.

'Good shot,' said Mrs Mandiddee, patting Billy on the back.

They waited, but nobody got out of the milk float. No friendly face looked up. In fact, to their horror they saw the milk float start up. It was leaving.

'No!' gasped Billy. 'You can't leave us here! Mrs M, what are we going to do?'

But she was one step ahead of him. 'Look out, Billy!'

He turned to see Mrs Mandiddee charging towards the window with the rolled-up not-so-magic carpet. He stepped aside and together they shoved it through the narrow window frame. Now it flew! Straight down, tassels flapping until, with a huge THUD, it landed right on the roof of the milk float.

CHAPTER 27

BUTTER

The milk float skidded to a halt.

'Up here,' said Billy in an exaggerated whisper. 'We need help.' He tried to sound like the kind of person who didn't normally throw carpets onto milk floats.

Eventually a milkman stepped out of the vehicle. Like all milkmen he wore a long, white jacket and a white peaked cap. Unlike all milkmen, he wasn't wearing any shoes. Just socks.

Billy was flabbergasted. Not in a million years had he expected his father to step out from the milk float. 'Dad! What are you doing here?'

'Looking for you.' Christopher Slipper tapped his finger on his forehead. 'What happened to your head?'

Billy touched his forehead. The marshmallows! Five were still stuck to him like limpets on a rock. A sixth had tangled in his hair and dangled about like a cork on an Australian hat.

'I thought I'd better come looking for you. Your mother is furious.'

Billy chose to ignore the bit about his mother. 'How did you find us?'

'I'm a milkman. I know where everyone lives. Where's the car?'

'We left it in a field,' explained Billy. It wasn't exactly a lie; they had left the car in a field. *How* it was left was a different matter altogether.

In between the loud snores, Billy explained what had happened, and how they had ended up as prisoners in the tower.

'Can you squeeze through the window?' asked Christopher Slipper. 'You could climb down using the ivy. It looks strong enough.'

'But my head's too big. I've tried. It won't fit,' said Billy.

'Wait a minute. I've got an idea.' Christopher Slipper scurried to the back of the milk float and rummaged. Moments later he pulled something out and held it above his head like a victorious athlete holding a trophy.

'What's he holding?' asked Mrs Mandiddee, squinting down.

'I think it's a packet of butter,' replied Billy.

'Why's he holding butter over his head?'

'I don't know.' He shrugged. His dad was behaving very strangely.

'I'm going to throw the butter up. Get ready to catch it,' said Christopher Slipper.

Billy's heart sunk. He had never been any good at catching. Once, at football practice he was put in goal. He let in seven goals in the first half alone and was never asked again. He stretched his arms through the window and hoped for the best.

'Here it comes!' Christopher Slipper arched back and threw the butter as hard as he could. It flew up and landed perfectly in Billy's cupped hands.

'Well caught!' said Mrs Mandiddee, clapping appreciatively.

'Now what?' asked Billy.

'Rub the butter all over your head,' called up Christopher Slipper.

Billy thought he'd misheard. Colonel Beauvrille's snoring was as loud as ever. 'What did you say?'

'Rub the butter all over your head. And put

some on your shoulders as well.'

'Why?'

'You'll see.'

Billy turned to Mrs Mandiddee. 'He wants me to cover my head and shoulders in butter.'

Without questioning, Mrs Mandiddee took the butter and peeled back the wrapper. 'Stand still now.' Like a mother applying suncream, she scooped out a dollop and began smearing it across Billy's face.

'You can tell me later why you've got marshmallows stuck to your head,' she added with a smile. 'Now close your eyes.'

She used the whole packet; a thick coating all over his head, his hair, down his neck and across his shoulders. Billy wiped a globule off the end of his nose and licked it. It was tasty. Now all he needed was a slice of toast.

He leant out of the window and waved at his dad. 'Now what?'

'Try to push your head through the window. It might slip through now.'

So that was the idea! Billy positioned himself up against the window and pushed. Ever so slowly, he slid forward. It felt like he was pulling a very tight jumper over his head. Halfway through, he stopped.

'Owww, my ears. I can't get my ears through.'

'Your ears!' shrieked Mrs Mandiddee. 'I forgot to butter your ears. Silly old me!'

She scooped a blob of butter off his shoulder and smeared it over his ears.

'Try that. And if it doesn't work we could always cut them off,' she said with a giggle. Normally Billy would have laughed, but it's hard to laugh with your head stuck halfway through a stone window.

Billy moved gently forward again. The tops of his ears folded back against his head as they scraped against the stone. He could hear the butter squelching through every fibre of his hair until, PING, his left ear sprung through, then, PONG, the right ear and then, at last, POP, his head was through.

The rest was easier. He turned his body and slid his buttered shoulders through the narrow gap. Then, with his arms tucked by his side, Mrs Mandiddee picked up his feet and pushed him, inch by inch through the window, the way you might stuff a parcel into a letterbox. As soon as his hands were free, Billy grabbed hold of the ivy above the window and pulled his legs through. With his feet on the window sill, Billy felt a flutter in his stomach. It was a very long way down.

What is the worst thing you can say to someone who is very high up?

'Don't look down,' advised Christopher Slipper.

Billy looked down. His legs went to jelly and beads of sweat bubbled through his buttery brow.

'Billy,' said Mrs Mandiddee calmly, 'look at me.'

In the small gap between his feet he saw Mrs

Mandiddee resting her head on the window sill. She looked up at him and grinned.

'Now what seems to be the problem?'

'I don't think I can move. It's too high.'

'Too high? Yes, I suppose you're right. You'd better come back in here, then.'

But he didn't want to go back in. He wanted to get to the bottom and see his dad. He wanted to rescue Jumblecat and get as far away from Deadham Castle as possible. Gradually, his legs stopped shaking and his stomach stopped churning. He smiled back at his best friend. Somehow, she always knew what to say and how to get the best out of him.

He inched his left foot off the sill and lowered it, feeling around for something that might take his weight. There! He found a small hole in the stonework, just enough to slip his shoe into. His other foot found an ivy branch. Billy tested it for strength, giving it a little push, before resting his weight on it. As long as he didn't look down he felt all right. When his foot found nothing beneath him, he inched sideways and sure enough there'd be another branch or nook to take his weight. This was easier than he thought.

He didn't notice the window to his left; the ivy

had completely grown over it. Nor did he notice that the snoring had stopped. And he certainly didn't see the thick, hairy arm emerging from the obscured window, and a huge, meaty hand with fingers outstretched, reaching towards him.

'Look out!' yelled Christopher Slipper.

But it was too late. Like a grape off a vine, Billy was plucked from the wall and violently hauled back into the gloom of Deadham Castle.

CHAPTER 28

THE ETERNITY POSE

It was as black as night. All Billy could hear was heavy breathing.

'Who is it?' He tried not to sound scared.

A blinding flash of red and yellow light lit up the room followed by a deep-purple glow.

'You remember the firefly beetle, don't you?' Colonel Beauvrille's giant, bearded face was only inches away. 'I was going to stuff it, but then it makes such a marvelleeus night light, don't you think?'

He pointed to the firefly beetle sitting in a jam jar on the dressing table.

Colonel Beauvrille held Billy by the back of his trousers, at arm's length, dangling him in mid-air like a mouse in a laboratory.

'Would you believe I'm scared of the dark? A man of my size! Ridiculous!'

Billy still clutched fistfuls of ivy ripped from the castle wall. 'Put me down,' he demanded.

'If you insist.'

Colonel Beauvrille was a tall man; it was a long drop. Billy landed heavily on the stone floor.

'Did that hurt?' asked Colonel Beauvrille, none too concerned.

Billy didn't answer. It did hurt, but he wasn't going to say so.

'I've been meaning to lay carpets on these floors for some years now. It would be so nice to get out of bed in the morning and put my feet on something warm and furry, don't you think? Maybe I should buy some slippers? Or make some? Jumblecat slippers!' He clapped his hands together with excitement. 'How does that sound? Hmmm, you're right, not very practical. All those legs sticking out in every direction. And there'd only be enough Jumblecat for one foot.'

Colonel Beauvrille sat down at his dressing table and began combing his beard. It reminded Billy of how Mindy would sit at her dressing table at home, endlessly combing her hair. For the first time in his life he wished his twin sister was with him now.

'Did you know, you and the twig lady are my first guests in fifteen years? It's so nice to have guests. Did you enjoy my hospitality? I pride myself on being an excellent host.' He had his back to Billy but, every now and again, glanced at him in the mirror. 'I would have brought you a morning cup of tea, but then I remembered you mustn't eat or drink twelve hours before your operation. Not a drop! I don't want you leaking Earl Grey all over my floor when I open you up.' Colonel Beauvrille thought this was hilarious and burst into one of his high-pitched giggles.

Billy gulped. He meant it. He really was planning to stuff him.

'Oh, don't worry. It's perfectly painless. And think, you'll never grow old. Just like Peter Pan. Without the flying and that irritating Darling family, of course.' He put down the beard comb and turned to face Billy. 'I'm glad you've dropped in, because I wanted to discuss with you your eternity pose.'

Billy spoke up for the first time. 'My eternity pose?'

'Let me explain. When I stuff you, you'll be in the same pose forever. I call it the eternity pose. As I've never stuffed a human specimen before, I want to get it right. I had thought of you holding your cat, you know, a boy and his cat, forever together. I can be rather sentimental, you see. But perhaps you'd like to be alone, holding a spear, a boy hunter.' Colonel Beauvrille stood up and pretended to be throwing a spear. 'What do you think?'

The man was mad. Here he was discussing Billy's 'eternity pose' as if it was the most normal thing in the world. He might as well have been discussing his favourite ice-cream flavour.

Billy needed time to think. Somehow he had to get out of here. The only door was on the other side of the room, right behind the colonel.

'Oh, don't get any ideas,' said Colonel Beauvrille, noticing Billy's wandering eyes. 'The door's locked. All the doors are locked and I've got the only key. That milkman can't get in, just as twig lady upstairs can't get out.' He cocked his head to one side like a dog. 'What strange company you keep!'

The firefly beetle bathed the room in deep orange. It made Colonel Beauvrille look badly sunburnt.

Just then Billy had an idea. Well, if the truth be told it was only half an idea, but that, he reckoned, was better than nothing. He stood up.

'What are you doing?' For a big man Colonel Beauvrille was very jittery.

'I've got an idea for my, er, eternity position.'

'Eternity pose, dear boy. It's called an eternity pose. Oh, how marvelleeus! What do you have in mind?'

'Erm, well, when I'm at home, I love dressing up. In costumes,' lied Billy. 'Especially with my sister, Mindy,' Billy double-lied.

Colonel Beauvrille frowned. 'What a hideous name. Mindy.' He rolled the name around on his tongue. 'Minnndy. Minnnnnndy. Sort of name you'd give a cockroach.'

At least they agreed on something.

Billy continued with his half-plan. 'For my eternity pose I want to look smart. Not these old clothes. I'd like to look like you, for example.'

If the room wasn't so orange, you'd have seen Colonel Beauvrille blush. 'Like me? But I only ever wear the same, boring thing,' he said with false modesty.

'But I think you look very . . . dignified.' Billy paused and took a deep breath. 'Do you think I could try your jacket on? Just to see?'

'Of course, dear boy. What a marvelleeus idea!' Colonel Beauvrille took off his jacket and held it open for Billy. 'It'll be far too big for you, but, please, be my guest.'

Billy put his arms into the sleeves and slipped on

183

the jacket. It weighed a ton and hung to the floor. He felt his knees buckling under the weight, but still managed to force a smile.

'I love it,' he grimaced.

'I've got hundreds of them,' said Colonel Beauvrille. He was delighted. 'I've worn exactly the same thing since I was a small boy. Look.'

He crossed the room and swung open the cupboard doors. Inside were rows and rows of tweed suits, ranging from small to giant size. He ran his enormous finger over the smallest one.

'This was my first ever tweed suit. My mother had it made for me when I was two. From that day on I never wore anything else.'

As Colonel Beauvrille reminisced, Billy plunged his hand into the jacket pocket and felt around. It was cavernous, more like a pillow case than a pocket. His fingers found some coins, a tweed handkerchief, but not what he was searching for.

And then, deep in the corner of the pocket, Billy struck gold. The key. The only key. The key he had seen Colonel Beauvrille use the night before. Billy gripped it tight in his hand and wondered what to do next. It was, after all, only half a plan.

'Maybe I can find a suit in your size,' said Colonel

Beauvrille, leaning into the cupboard. 'Oh, you *will* look smart. I can't wait to stuff you.'

As Colonel Beauvrille leant deeper into the cupboard, Billy took a chance. He slipped off the jacket and charged at Colonel Beauvrille, hammering into his legs. It was like a pea hitting an anvil, imperceptible, but somehow it was just enough to knock the big man off balance. Colonel Beauvrille wobbled and swayed and with an almighty crash, toppled over into the cupboard, collapsing under an avalanche of tweed.

He roared. Not in pain but in fury. 'Wait till I get my hands on –'

Billy slammed the cupboard shut, ran to the door and with shaking hands, tried putting the key in the lock.

'Come on, Billy. Come on, Billy,' he said to himself.

Colonel Beauvrille kicked down the cupboard doors. They flew off their hinges, crashing to the floor. Waistcoats and trousers and jackets flew out as Colonel Beauvrille struggled to unearth himself. It was like a volcano of tweed erupting across the room. Finally, Billy managed to get the key in. With shaking hands he unlocked the door and . . .

THWACK! Colonel Beauvrille clapped his massive hands around Billy's head and lifted him clear off the floor. Billy's legs danced and dangled in the air like a helpless puppet.

'Oh, I'm going to enjoy stuffing you,' snorted Colonel Beauvrille, squeezing Billy's head far too hard.

Billy felt his jawbone creak. His eyeballs wanted to pop out. His head was about to explode.

How could Colonel Beauvrille have known that Billy's head was covered in greasy, slimy butter? As he increased the pressure, his hands skidded off and, in an enormous two-fisted punch, flew up into his face, knocking himself clean out.

For the second time, Billy fell to the floor.

Next to him lay Colonel Beauvrille, flat out on a nest of tweed.

CHAPTER 29

TINY, TWIGGY AND MILKY

Billy locked the door behind him and raced up the tower stairs. He unlocked the door and freed Mrs Mandiddee. Quickly, he told her what had happened.

'You knocked him out?' she shrieked.

'I think so,' replied Billy. 'Well, he knocked himself out, really.'

'Good for you. He's nothing but an overgrown bully.'

They hurried back down the tower and along the corridor of ugly ancestors. As they passed by the taxidermist's tea party, Billy suddenly stopped and sniffed the air. 'What's that smell?' he asked. 'It's delicious.'

Mrs Mandiddee pointed at a large, silver tray in the centre of the table. It was filled with the most mouth-watering breakfast foods; from exotic fruits to bacon, sausages, poached eggs, fried bread, the works. 'Colonel Beauvrille's been busy,' she said. 'It's a breakfast party. And look! The animals! They're all different.'

She was right. Arranged around the table was a completely new set of animals. The pig, octopus and horse had all gone. Now a lioness wearing velvet gloves sat at the head of the table. Next to her, where the chicken once sat, was a mole dressed in a choirboy's ruff. Perched opposite, taking up three spaces, was the swan with the outstretched wings that Billy had seen in the book *Castles of England*. There was a walrus drinking wine, an otter sniffing at a bottle of brown sauce and a strange-looking bird, with a large hooked beak.

'It's a dodo,' said Mrs Mandiddee. 'It must be the one Colonel Beauvrille was talking about. The last ever dodo, stuffed by his great-grandfather.'

Billy took a closer look. It had a toupee on its head and looked rather miserable. Unlike the other animals, its plate was empty.

'Do you think Colonel Beauvrille eats with different animals every day?' asked Mrs Mandiddee.

But Billy had seen enough. 'Let's go. I think I know where to find Jumblecat.'

Christopher Slipper was waiting anxiously in his milk float.

'Thank goodness you're all right,' he said happily, giving Billy the biggest hug.

'Dad. I'm OK.'

'I tried to get in, but everything's locked. I was about to go for help,' said Christopher Slipper, still squeezing his son.

'Dad. I'm fine.'

Just then, a bloodcurdling roar came from Colonel Beauvrille's dressing room. He'd come round with an enormous headache. He lay on the floor trying to piece together what had happened; why his head hurt so badly, why his hands were so oily, why he was half buried in tweed . . . and then he remembered . . . 'Why, that snivelling little runt. I'll throttle him.'

He steadied himself against the dressing table. His head throbbed and pounded. In his army days he had been something of a boxing champion, but nobody had ever hit him like this. He tried the door but it was locked. He stumbled over to the window and pulled aside the curtain of ivy. 'Oh, there you all are. How delightful. The three musketeers: Tiny, Twiggy and Milky. Do you know what I'm going to do to you when I get out of here?' He didn't wait for an answer. 'I'm going to stuff you alive, one by one, then rip you apart, bit by bit and feed you to the birds. And if the birds don't eat you, I'll feed you to the fish. You'll make marvelleeus fish food.' He squeezed his fat arm through the window and pointed a finger at Billy. 'And you. I'll save you until last. Aren't I kind? Will you excuse me now?

I must go and break down the door.'

All they could hear was THUMP THUMP THUMP as Colonel Beauvrille charged at the door again and again and again, like a deranged animal battering the bars of a cage.

There was no time to waste. Billy hurried across the courtyard and put the key in the same door he'd seen Colonel Beauvrille open the night before.

'Where are you going?' cried Christopher Slipper. 'We've got to get out of here.'

'But Jumblecat's in here. I'm sure of it,' said Billy, turning the key.

'He's right, Billy, we should go,' insisted Mrs Mandiddee. Another huge THUMP shook the castle walls. 'That door's not going to hold for much longer.'

Ninety-nine times out of a hundred, Billy would have listened to Mrs Mandiddee, but not this time. He wasn't leaving without Jumblecat.

'Give me five minutes. Please.'

Christopher Slipper looked at his son. 'Five minutes. And if you're not back by then, cat or no cat, I'm going to drag you out.'

CHAPTER 30

A TAXIDERMIST'S PARADISE

Billy opened the door and peered in. A short flight of stairs led down into a cellar. It was hot and smelly like a bowl of rotten vegetable soup.

'Jumblecat!' he called. There was no reply.

It was like any old cellar. Dusty shelves full of empty jam jars and plastic bottles with peeling labels. On the floor were sacks of tired-looking vegetables; potatoes, onions, cabbages, all well past their best. Billy ducked under a low wooden beam and passed through into the far end of the cellar. More shelves, more jam jars full of old nails, more tools covered in long abandoned cobwebs. In the far corner was an old-fashioned child's bed, with an arched headboard and thin metal legs. The bed was perfectly made up. There was even a raggedy old teddy bear waiting on the pillow for someone to come to bed. But no Jumblecat.

Billy could hear the muffled thump, thump, thump as Colonel Beauvrille did his utmost to break down the dressing-room door. Before too long it would splinter into a thousand pieces and the madman would be free. Billy sat down on the bed feeling drained and wretched. He'd made a promise to look after Jumblecat and he'd failed. Like the dodo, Jumblecat would become nothing more than a plaything at Colonel Beauvrille's table. Perhaps it would have been better if someone else had found Jumblecat at the bottom of Tumbledown Hill that day, someone who could have looked after him properly. His mother was right, he was just a silly boy who brought garbage into the house, cluttering up his bedroom. He pictured his Collectabillya sprawled across his floor. All worthless, like everything in this cellar.

'Billy!' called his dad from the top of the stairs. 'We've got to get going. Hurry up!'

That was it. It was time to go home. Without Jumblecat.

As Billy got up from the bed a fat moth fluttered

up off the pillow and bumbled haphazardly about the cellar, before landing on a tattered curtain that hung at the far end of the bed.

'A curtain? Cellars don't have curtains,' he said to himself. He prodded the curtain with his thumb. It was hard behind. The moth flew up, fluttering about his face. Billy slowly drew the curtain back, revealing a shiny metal door. As far as he could see there was no handle or keyhole, so he pushed against it with his shoulder.

It swung open easily.

Billy stepped into a large, circular chamber, powerfully lit by rows of strip lights that hung from the ceiling. The floor was laid with white marble and in the centre stood a wide stainless-steel table covered with scalpels and saws with razor-sharp teeth, tough enough to cut through bone. Everything was immaculate, cold and sterile. A taxidermist's paradise.

All around the curved walls were cages, dozens of them, each with thick steel bars. Almost every cage was occupied: rabbits, an ostrich, a tiger, meerkats, a koala. Just about every creature he could think of was here behind bars.

Not one of the animals made a sound. They were

lifeless, staring blankly at Billy. Looking, but not seeing.

He saw the knitting monkey sitting motionless in its cage. The monkey looked right through him as if he wasn't there. The lively, brilliant creature he remembered from the competition was nothing more than an empty shell. In the next cage was the tiny hippo. Billy pushed his finger between the bars. 'Hello, little thing,' he whispered, willing it to respond. But the hippo just sat there, staring back with glazed, dead eyes.

Then, at last, Billy found what he was looking for. 'Jumblecat!'

Nothing. No response. It was as though Billy was invisible.

He felt sick. He was too late. Jumblecat wasn't Jumblecat any more; he was just another stuffed animal in Colonel Beauvrille's collection.

Billy lifted the latch and opened the cage door. Whatever Colonel Beauvrille had done to Jumblecat, there was no way he was going to leave him here. 'I've come to get you out of here,' said Billy, determined not to cry. 'I'm taking you home.'

Just then, as he reached into the cage, Billy realised that something didn't make sense. If

Jumblecat had been stuffed, then why was he still being kept in a cage – he was hardly likely to escape if he'd already been stuffed full of newspaper or tummy button fluff? Right now Jumblecat should be sitting at Colonel Beauvrille's breakfast table with all the other stuffed animals. It just didn't add up.

Billy felt his heart beating more rapidly. Hardly daring to hope, he gently placed his hand onto Jumblecat's tummy.

He was still warm.

'Jumblecat! Can you hear me? It's me, Billy. Billy Slipper.'

He picked up one of Jumblecat's legs and gave it a squeeze. But Jumblecat didn't react. The leg slipped out of Billy's hand and flopped lifelessly back down.

'What's wrong with you? Wake up!'

Billy crawled into the cage, put his head next to Jumblecat's tummy and listened for a heartbeat. He had no idea where a cat's heart was, less so on a jumbled-up cat, but nonetheless, he closed his eyes and concentrated as hard as he could. 'Come on, come on, where is it?' he said to himself, pushing his ear closer to the ginger fur.

As Billy shifted about, the marshmallow-tangled-in-his-hair rolled off the top of his head and dangled tantalisingly in front of Jumblecat's nose. The nose twitched. Then Jumblecat's tongue darted out of his mouth, the tip of it jabbing the marshmallow, sending it swinging from side to side. Moments later, as if in a giant yawn, Jumblecat's mouth began to open, wider and wider and wider, before SNAP, clamping down around the soft, pink marshmallow.

Billy jumped up, cracking the back of his head against the roof of the cage. 'Owwww!' he yelled.

'Mmmmm,' said Jumblecat, indifferent to Billy's pain, 'this tastes *good*.'

Billy backed out of the cage, rubbing his head. 'Jumblecat! You're alive!'

'Of course I'm alive. Now, what else have you got? I'm starving.'

'I thought you'd been stuffed. You weren't moving and I couldn't hear a heartbeat and . . .'

'Yeah, yeah, yeah,' interrupted Jumblecat. 'Look, I'm traumatised. I need to eat. Now!'

Billy picked up Jumblecat and kissed him.

Jumblecat sniffed at another marshmallow that was glued onto Billy's forehead and took a bite.

It was still the same old cat.

It took less than a minute to open all the cage doors, but not one of the animals moved.

Billy climbed up onto the stainless-steel table and begged them. 'Please! Come on! You're free! You can't stay here.' He banged his foot down hard on the table. The noise echoed fiercely around the chamber, but not one of the creatures flinched.

Christopher Slipper appeared in the doorway. 'Billy, we've got to go, now.'

'Dad, they won't move. What's wrong with them?'

'We can't wait any longer, Billy.'

'But . . .' Billy's eyes filled with tears, but his dad

was right. They had to go.

Billy got down and picked up Jumblecat. 'Please! Go!' he pleaded sadly one last time. But it was no good. All the animals remained stiff as statues.

Christopher Slipper put his arm around his son. 'There's nothing more you can do. They're probably sedated and we can't carry them all.'

'But Jumblecat woke up – why won't the others?' He looked down at Jumblecat who was busy licking at a splodge of marshmallow stuck to the end of his nose. All of a sudden, Billy's eyes glistened as bright as stars. 'That's it!' he cried. 'The marshmallows!

'What about the marshmallows?' asked Christopher Slipper.

'The smell of the marshmallows woke Jumblecat up. I'm sure of it.' Billy could hardly contain his excitement. 'Maybe we can wake the others up after all. We need more marshmallows.' Frantically he began patting his head. 'Dad, quick, are there any more marshmallows stuck on me?'

Christopher Slipper took his son's head in his hands and rummaged through his hair. 'I can't see any. Turn around.'

'Don't bother looking. I've eaten them all,' said Jumblecat lazily. 'And there was a hair in one of them. Disgusting! I practically choked.'

But Billy wasn't listening to Jumblecat. Already his brain was fizzing and buzzing and crackling with far-fetched ideas as to how to get the other animals to wake up.

Suddenly, one idea popped into his head that seemed less ridiculous than the others. 'It might just work!' he cried, thrusting Jumblecat into Christopher Slipper's arms. 'I'll be back in a minute, Dad, I promise.'

And before Christopher Slipper could stop him, Billy was off, racing through the cellar, up the stairs and out into the courtyard.

'Did you find Jumblecat?' shrieked Mrs Mandiddee as Billy rushed past her.

'Yes! We got him. He's OK.'

'Where are you going, then?'

There was no time to explain. Billy shot across the courtyard, skidding to a halt outside door number eleven. Inside, the taxidermist's breakfast party was still in full swing. Billy squeezed in between the swan and the walrus, reached over and picked up the large, silver tray full of amazing-smelling breakfast goodies. Too good to resist. Billy stuffed a sausage in his mouth and ran back outside, carrying the large tray in front of him.

As he passed Mrs Mandiddee again, she asked, quite reasonably, 'Can someone please tell me what's going on?'

With a sausage stuffed in his gob, Billy couldn't really tell her anything. 'Karrrfflop,' he managed to splutter, spraying sausage bits across the gravel. He was trying to say, 'Can't stop,' but there was no way Mrs Mandiddee could understand that.

'Karrrfflop? What?' she called out after him. 'Anyhow, can't breakfast wait?'

But already Billy was flying down the cellar stairs, two at a time, rashers and bangers bouncing around the tray as he ducked under the low beam and back into the taxidermy chamber.

'Have you lost your mind?' howled Christopher Slipper when he saw the breakfast tray. 'We need to get out of here, not eat!'

An enormous, muffled THUMP shook the whole underground chamber.

'Please, Dad. I know it'll work,' Billy said, setting the tray down on the stainless-steel table. 'Just give it a minute.'

The chamber quickly filled with an array of rich, meaty, eggy, fruity aromas. Billy flapped his hands around, wafting the delicious smells every which way.

A large dollop of drool dangled pendulously from Jumblecat's mouth. 'I can't take it any longer. Give me a sausage,' he miaow-moaned.

'Sssshhh!' said Billy. 'Look!' And for once, Jumblecat listened, because miraculously the animals were beginning to wake up. The knitting monkey was first, nose twitching, eyes flickering into life.

'It's working!' cried Christopher Slipper. 'Billy, you're a genius.'

The monkey stretched out his lanky arms and scratched his hairy bottom. Yawning noisily, he stumbled out of his cage and padded towards the tray of food. Billy scooped up a poached egg and put it in the monkey's hand.

'Do monkeys eat eggs?' asked Christopher Slipper.

'I'll have it if he doesn't want it,' offered Jumblecat.

The monkey rolled the rubbery egg around his nimble fingers, sniffed it and then popped it whole into his mouth.

Gradually, all the other animals started to show signs of life. The rabbits scratched. The tiny hippo snorted. The ostrich ruffled her feathers. One by one they stepped gingerly out of their cages.

'I'll lead the way,' said Christopher Slipper, taking

hold of the knitting monkey's hand. 'Billy, you bring up the rear.'

Excited animal chatter began to fill the chamber. Billy began herding them towards the exit. 'That's right. Keep going. Come on, meerkats. Don't push, tiger! Follow the milkman. It's all right, he's my dad.'

Steadily, they cleared the chamber. Only the tiny hippo was left, too small to climb out of the cage by himself. Billy scooped him up in the palm of his hand and headed for the stairs.

It was the most breathtaking spectacle: dozens of delirious creatures careering about the courtyard, celebrating their freedom. The ostrich charged around chased by gregarious rabbits. The kangaroo double-somersaulted high into the air. The knitting monkey climbed onto the roof of the Rolls-Royce and beat his chest. A balding Alsatian barked excitedly and chased its tail. An eagle and a parrot swooped over the castle, bombing and swerving around the tower and the tiger roared proudly and ran under the open portcullis into the countryside beyond. From the top step of the cellar Billy stood and watched the merry chaos. If there had ever been a party on Noah's Ark, it might have looked something like this.

CHAPTER 31

THE PORTCULLIS

From inside the castle there came an almighty CRASH. Colonel Beauvrille was out. The party was over.

Mrs Mandiddee flapped her arms about, herding the animals under the portcullis. 'Go on. Hop it! All of you. Sling yer hook! Get out of here. Now!'

Billy and his dad crammed as many creatures as they could into the milk float. Jumblecat on the front seat with the tiny hippo, the koala and red squirrel in the back, meerkats in the milk crates and raccoons in the butter fridge. The knitting monkey bounded off the Rolls-Royce and squeezed in next to Jumblecat.

Suddenly there was a terrible sound of heavy

metal chains unravelling.

'What's that noise?' shrieked Mrs Mandiddee.

Christopher Slipper pointed at the portcullis, which was now slowly descending, shutting off the only way out of the castle.

Quick as a shot, he leapt into the milk float and slammed his foot on the accelerator but milk floats are not built for speed, especially ones laden with animals. Billy ran behind and pushed with all his might.

'We'll never make it,' yelled Christopher Slipper.

He was right. Already the portcullis was halfway down.

Colonel Beauville stepped into the courtyard, calmly watching the unfolding spectacle. There was no other way out of Deadham Castle and he knew it. As soon as the portcullis was down he'd have all the time in the world to carry out his revenge. And besides, he was enjoying watching them panic.

'Oh dear. Did I activate the portcullis? Silly old me. You all seem to be in a bit of trouble. Can I be of any assistance?' He could hardly contain his giggles.

Mrs Mandiddee ran ahead of the milk float and stood beneath the portcullis. She grabbed hold of it and tried pushing it back up. Her elderly, withered muscles quivered but the portcullis continued its slow, inevitable descent, forcing her to her knees. How could she stop it? After all, she was well over ninety years old and couldn't even hold a tray of tea without spilling most of it.

And then the most incredible thing happened.

Sometimes, in newspapers or on television, there are stories of people performing acts of superhuman strength under extreme circumstances; a mother lifting a car when her baby is trapped underneath or an old lady fighting off a gang of robbers with only her handbag – that sort of thing. It can't be explained.

What happened next *certainly* can't be explained. It just happened.

The sight of this scrawny old woman attempting to raise the portcullis tickled Colonel Beauvrille no end.

'Oh bravo!' he said, applauding sarcastically. 'That's the spirit. Heave!'

She glared across the courtyard at her tormentor. Her face went the colour of beetroot and her cheeks rippled with rage.

'I always knew it would have been a waste of time

stuffing you. Just as I thought, leaves and twigs. That's all you're made of, leaves and twigs,' he taunted.

But with every word of mockery, with every provocative syllable, Mrs Mandiddee felt herself growing stronger and stronger. If Colonel Beauvrille had realised this, he would have shut up there and then. But he didn't.

'That's right, dear, let the portcullis crush you. It'll save me the bother of having to make a bonfire to burn you up, twig lady.'

That was it. The final straw. Mrs Mandiddee heaved with all her might and miraculously, the portcullis ground to a halt. She got up from her knees onto her feet. The mechanism clunked and groaned in protest. Her arms locked; her shoulders became boulders and inch by inch, the portcullis started to rise. With her arms at full stretch above her head, Mrs Mandiddee exploded into hysterical laughter as if what she was doing was the easiest thing in the world, as if she was holding just a bag of feathers above her head.

'Well, don't just stand there!' she boomed. 'Get that thing out of here.'

Christopher Slipper did as he was told. The teeth of the portcullis clawed the roof of the milk float as it squeezed underneath.

'That's everyone,' said Billy hurriedly. 'You can put it down now.'

But Mrs Mandiddee didn't put it down.

'Mrs M. Let it go.'

She wasn't listening. She was like a matador; strong and without fear. She locked eyes with Colonel Beauvrille. 'Come on, bully boy. Come and get me,' she taunted. 'Are you frightened of the twig lady?' Her voice grew stronger. 'I think you're just a great big lump of scaredy-cat jelly.'

Nobody had ever called Colonel Beauvrille scaredy-cat jelly before. He snorted like a bull and scraped his foot across the gravel, kicking up a cloud of dust. Sweat dripped from his forehead, stinging his eyes. His whole body twitched uncontrollably as he prepared to charge.

'You'll regret this,' he snarled. 'I'll make you wish you never came to Deadham Castle.'

And then, with a bovine roar, he charged. For a big man he moved surprisingly fast. Within seconds he was halfway across the courtyard and gaining speed.

Billy pleaded with Mrs Mandiddee. 'What are you doing? Please, let go of the portcullis!'

She held fast. Colonel Beauvrille rampaged closer. Frenzied, tattered tweed suit, hair frothing; he was the Wild Beast of Deadham Castle. He could see the whites of Mrs Mandiddee's eyes and the wrinkles on her neck, the same neck he was moments from throttling. As Colonel Beauvrille extended his arms towards her, she stepped back and let the portcullis drop.

For the second time that day, Colonel Beauvrille knocked himself out. He slammed into the portcullis with such force, an impression of his body embedded in the five-hundred-year-old metal.

Mrs Mandiddee looked down at the unconscious bundle of tweed and beard. 'Not bad for a bunch of leaves and twigs,' she said, dusting off her hands. 'Not bad at all.'

CHAPTER 32

A LEOPARD AND A SNAIL

The countryside fizzed with life. Wild flowers stretched up towards the sun, birds darted in and out of unkempt hedgerows and giant oak trees swayed in the summer breeze in perfect time with the long grass.

Piled high with exotic creatures, the milk float resembled a travelling circus going from village to village. Passing cars slowed right down to get a better look. Some honked their horns and waved. Billy waved back. He couldn't remember feeling so happy. Not only had he rescued Jumblecat, but he'd done it with his best friend and his dad; his crew of bloodthirsty pirates! He looked over at Mrs Mandiddee, fast asleep, resting her head on the knitting monkey's shoulder. She seemed so frail, a little old lady. It was hard to imagine that only moments ago, she had lifted something ten times her weight. Between them sat Jumblecat, licking his paws. He really was an odd-looking thing; as if drawn by a child with a bizarre sense of humour. Billy stroked what he hoped was his tummy.

'I suppose you want me to say thank you for rescuing me,' said Jumblecat.

Billy shrugged his shoulders. Incredibly, it was the first time that Jumblecat had even acknowledged that Billy had done anything for him. It was, in Jumblecat's roundabout way, a kind of thank you. Billy sat back and smiled.

'That doesn't mean you can stop stroking my tummy,' insisted Jumblecat.

So Billy kept stroking until Jumblecat drifted off to sleep. Billy was tired too, but he was determined to stay awake. He wanted to remember every detail of this journey; the playful grunts of the tiny hippo as the monkey tickled his leathery snout and the sound of Mrs Mandiddee's gentle snoring. He wanted to remember how his dad's wedding ring sparkled in the sun as he turned the steering wheel. He wanted to remember how happy he felt, because these are the moments that never grow old.

'Billy. Wake up!'

Billy opened his eyes. For a moment he had no idea what he was doing on a milk float trundling through the countryside with a monkey asleep in his lap.

'What's going on?' he said groggily.

'We've got company,' said Christopher Slipper, pointing over his shoulder.

Billy looked round. There was nothing behind them; just a quiet country road drifting away into the evening sun. Mrs Mandiddee woke up too. 'What are you looking at?' she asked.

Just then a black Rolls-Royce screeched around the corner and accelerated at ferocious speed towards them. Imagine a leopard chasing a snail; the chase was over in seconds. Colonel Beauvrille stuck his head out of his window. His beard flapped about his face like a kite stuck in a treetop.

'What a surprise, meeting you out here,' he bellowed, 'and on such a pleasant evening too.' His face was bruised and battered and a huge cartoon lump protruded out of his forehead. 'Could you kindly pull over? I want a pint of milk.

Semi-skimmed will do,' he said, giggling like a naughty schoolgirl in church.

Of course, Christopher Slipper kept going as fast as he could, which was not very fast at all.

Colonel Beauvrille was enjoying himself. 'No milk today? That *is* a shame. And I so wanted a cup of cocoa before bed. Oh well, I'll have to milk the cow myself.' He put his foot down on the accelerator and charged.

'Hold on!' yelled Christopher Slipper, as the Rolls-Royce slammed into them. The back of the milk float flew up into the air and landed with a colossal thud. Milk crates crashed around the back, a meerkat flew out onto the soft grass verge, the monkey tumbled on top of Jumblecat, but somehow, Christopher Slipper managed to stay on the road.

Billy wasn't scared, he was furious. He hadn't come all this way to be run off the road by a lunatic. 'Just keep driving,' he said to his dad and climbed over his seat into the back of the milk float.

Colonel Beauvrille was ranting again. 'I only want the cat. The rest of you can go back to your little homes and your little lives. Give me the cat.'

Billy picked up a milk bottle that was rolling around his feet. 'Jumblecat's mine,' he shouted, hurling the bottle as hard as he could at the Rolls-Royce. It smashed on the car bonnet, spraying milk and glass all over the windscreen.

Colonel Beauvrille switched on the wipers. 'I thought I asked for semi-skimmed. That looks too creamy for me. I've got to watch my figure. Doctor's orders!' And with just the slightest touch on the accelerator, he rammed the milk float again. 'Whoops-a-daisy.'

Billy was thrown sideways and fell to the floor. The doors of the butter fridge flew open, spewing raccoons and butter into the air. Orange juice and milk flooded everywhere, slooshing this way and that as the milk float weaved unsteadily across the road.

'Are you OK?' hollered Mrs Mandiddee.

'Never better,' replied Billy, staggering to his feet. 'Would you like to join me?'

As if she had just received an invitation to the best party in town, she climbed over the front seat and took her position by Billy's side.

'Ready?' he asked.

'Ready,' she replied, picking up four packets of butter.

'Take aim. Fire!'

Orange juice, butter and milk rained down onto Colonel Beauvrille's car, splashing orange, yellow and white all over the shiny black paint. Colonel Beauvrille turned the windscreen wipers up to maximum, weathering the dairy storm. Sooner or later they'd run out of things to throw and when that moment came, he'd ram the milk float off the road and the cat would be his.

He didn't have to wait long. Apart from a half-eaten packet of butter (the raccoons had got hungry), the back of the milk float was empty. There was nothing else to throw.

Colonel Beauvrille stuck his head out of the window again. 'Have you quite finished? Good. Now it's my turn.' He revved the engine.

It was his last chance. Billy dived to the floor, scooped up the half-packet of butter and hurled it as hard as he could.

It was the perfect shot, splatting Colonel Beauvrille right in the eyes. 'I can't see!' he wailed. 'Help!'

The sleek, black Rolls-Royce veered off the road and smashed through a fence. It looked like a giant metallic slug, scything through the long grass towards the river at the bottom. Colonel Beauvrille, blinded by butter (and a little raccoon spit), felt the car getting faster and faster, careering down the hill.

The Rolls-Royce plunged into the water with all the elegance of a breeze block. Great waves splashed over the riverbanks as the car floated off downstream.

'Where does that river go?' asked Billy.

'All the way out to the sea,' replied his dad cheerfully as he urged the milk float on. 'Now, let's get home!'

CHAPTER 33

EUREKA

By the time they got into town it was very late. The
wind had picked up and the first spots of rain were
falling. The streets were deserted; the town was
sleeping. A fox strutted across the road in front of
them. It turned and stared, eyes glinting yellow in
the headlights, then trotted off. They passed the
Old Grand Hall. Billy had never seen it at night.
Spotlights lit up each column and the glass dome
was illuminated from the inside by a pale, creamy
light. More than ever it looked like a solitary jellyfish
drifting through the night sea.

Christopher Slipper turned onto the road that led
to the edge of town and home. Nobody spoke, but
everyone was thinking the same thing: Phillipa Slipper.

How do you explain: stealing the car, abandoning the smashed-up car in a field, bringing back the cat she had already sold, a milk float awash with orangey milk and raccoon poo, a defiant husband, a disobedient son, a neighbour she never liked in the first place and a small menagerie of curious animals?

In other words, she wasn't going to be pleased.

The milk float turned off the main road and pulled up outside Mrs Mandiddee's house.

'You could all stay here until this blows over,' she suggested. 'I'm sure things will settle down soon enough.'

But she knew as well as the rest of them that Phillipa Slipper was not the forgiving kind. It was well known that she held lifelong grudges against most people in town; the greengrocer for his overpriced plums, the librarian for daring to ask her to keep her voice down, children for being too young. She was *never* going to forgive or forget about this.

The rain was really coming down now, hammering on the roof of the milk float. Nobody got out. It was as if the rain was protecting them from all the problems they would soon have to deal with. As long as they were sitting out here, under cover, nothing could harm them, they were safe. They huddled closer together. Billy wished it would rain forever, because, as far as he could tell, there could never be a happy ending.

Sometimes, when faced with an enormous problem, an idea will spring into your mind that is so blindingly obvious, so brilliant, you wonder why you never thought of it in the first place. It's called a 'eureka moment' and is often accompanied by an 'A-haaa', as if to say, 'I've got it. I know the answer.'

'A-haaa,' said Billy, grinning from ear to ear.

'What is it?' asked Mrs Mandiddee.

'It might just work,' replied Billy, not answering her question. He turned to his dad. 'Can the milk float go cross-country?'

Christopher Slipper looked out at the pouring rain. 'I'm not sure. I've only ever driven it on the road. Why?'

Billy's eyes shined with excitement. 'Can we try?'

'Where to?'

'Do you know the way to the top of Tumbledown Hill?'

'Of course I do,' he replied, starting up the milk float. He switched on the windscreen wipers and peered out into the storm. 'It's going to be muddy.'

A flash of lightning lit up the whole street. Christopher Slipper turned the milk float around and headed towards Tumbledown Hill.

Mindy couldn't sleep. Believe it or not, she missed Billy. Her twin brother might have been the most idiotic person in the world, but at night-time, she realised she liked having him around. There were too many shadows. Too many noises. She imagined the hair-singed cellar dolls plotting their revenge and creeping into her room to cut off her precious hair with blunt scissors. And now, of all things, she heard voices coming from outside.

'The cellar dolls! They're coming to get me!' she wailed, pulling her duvet up to her chin. She lay there without moving a muscle, listening to the muffled voices coming from the street. The curtains billowed gently as the rain got heavier. The window! It was open! What if the dolls climbed up the drainpipe and in through the open window? Unless she closed it straight away she would be bald by morning. Summoning all her courage, she slipped out of bed and peeked through the gap in the curtains.

The rain was coming down in buckets, but as far as she could see there were no cellar dolls brandishing scissors outside her window. A huge flash of lightning filled the sky. And that's when she saw the milk float.

'Muuuuuum!' she yelled at the top of her whiney voice. 'They're back!'

Halfway up Tumbledown Hill the milk float shuddered like an old washing machine and finally expired. It had had enough. Milk floats are only designed to trundle along smooth roads at a sedate pace, not act as getaway vehicles or cross-country menageries. Billy got out and pushed, but it was no good; the hill was too steep and the grass too slippery. They would have to walk.

Billy led the way followed by Christopher Slipper, who carried Jumblecat rolled up in his white milk-delivery coat. Mrs Mandiddee brought up the rear. The rain lashed into their faces and the thunder seemed to shake the ground beneath them.

'Don't you have an umbrella?' moaned Jumblecat. 'I'm not a cat who likes getting wet.'

'And I'm not a milkman who likes carrying fat cats,' replied Christopher Slipper. 'You can walk if you like.' He wasn't joking.

Jumblecat kept quiet after that.

If anyone had seen this strange party climbing Tumbledown Hill during a raging storm in the middle of the night they would have thought they were seeing things. A milkman, a geriatric and a boy, a jumbled-up cat poking out from a white coat, meerkats, a koala, raccoons, a balding Alsatian, a monkey, all struggling up the soggy hillside. It was hardly your usual Sunday-afternoon outing.

Great squalls of wind lashed the rain into their faces and soaked them to the skin. 'What's the plan?' shouted Mrs Mandiddee through the storm. The wind was threatening to blow her off her feet. Billy thought he should tie a piece of string to her arm in case she blew away.

'I'll tell you when we get to the top.' The truth was, Billy was beginning to doubt if his plan would work at all. The more he thought about it, the more it seemed too ridiculously simple. He crossed his fingers for luck and ducked his head down against the driving rain.

CHAPTER 34

A CAT LIKE ANY OTHER CAT

'I won't do it!' protested Jumblecat.

Billy tried to sound as convincing as possible. 'It'll work. I'm sure of it.'

'You expect me to throw myself down the hill.'

'I can give you a little push, just to get you going. And when you reach the bottom, you'll be fixed. No more jumbled-up cat.'

Jumblecat craned his neck and looked down the steep slope. 'That's the most stupid thing I've ever heard in my life. By the time I reach the bottom I'll be exactly the same as I am now, except scratched and bruised.'

'But that's just it,' persisted Billy. 'When I found you, there wasn't a scratch or bruise on you. Don't you remember? You weren't hurt, you were just jumbled up. If you go down again, you'll be fixed. And it won't hurt, I promise.'

Jumblecat looked up at Mrs Mandiddee. 'Did you know your friend is totally barmy? He's dragged us all the way up here in a raging storm. I'm soaked. You're soaked. And for what? To throw me down the hill again! I'd rather eat my own tail.'

'Please, Jumblecat,' pleaded Billy.

'And stop calling me that. It's a stupid name. Can't you call me something normal, like Simon or Colin?'

It crossed Billy's mind to pick up the obstinate cat and just throw him down the hill there and then.

Mrs Mandiddee tried a different approach. 'I'll buy you as many biscuits as you want. Just think of it – custard creams, Bourbons, chocolate digestives.'

His whiskers twitched, but he remained defiant. 'No way.'

Just as Mrs Mandiddee considered picking up the obstinate cat and throwing him down the hill, she saw something. It looked like a ghost, all in white, gliding through the stormy night. She wiped the rain from her eyes and squinted down into the valley. Whatever it was, it was moving fast and heading towards them.

'Look,' she pointed. 'What's that?'

An enormous flash of lightning streaked through the night sky, lighting up the whole valley. It was no ghost. More horrifying than a ghost.

It was Phillipa Slipper.

She pounded barefoot across the field, wearing only her white nightdress. Her long brown hair, loose and wet, slapped against her face. Above her head she brandished a spatula, waving it around like a samurai sword. She looked every inch the demented warrior, hunting down her prey.

In no time at all she reached the milk float. Finding it empty, she scraped the hair from her face and glared up to the top of the hill. 'BILLY SLIPPER!' she roared. 'YOU ARE IN BIG TROUBLE!'

A shiver ran down Billy's spine. He had seen his mother cross, angry, furious, even eye-poppingly livid, but never anything like this. His first instinct was to run – whose wouldn't be? – but he couldn't leave Jumblecat now.

And then something happened that Billy never expected to see. His dad, the quiet milkman, who never said boo to a goose, marched down the hill towards his enraged wife.

'Dad! What are you doing?'

Christopher Slipper didn't answer. He simply raised his arm as if to say, 'Don't worry, son, I'll sort this out.'

Billy held his breath. He'd never seen his dad stand up to his mum before. All his life he'd only seen her telling him off, telling him what to do, belittling him. For a brief moment he imagined them as young and happy, running towards each other on the side of a windswept hill. For a brief, blissful moment he imagined them falling into a happy embrace, followed by tears, apologies and a nice cup of tea. He remembered his wish the night the shooting star flew over his back garden. Maybe it would come true after all . . .

Silly Billy. Christopher Slipper never stood a chance. Without even breaking her stride, Phillipa Slipper slammed into him, knocking him over like a skittle in a bowling alley. Her sights were firmly set on her delinquent son and nothing was going to stand in her way.

Billy crouched in the wet grass beside Jumblecat and awaited his fate. There was nothing else he could do. He'd tried his absolute best to help Jumblecat, but had failed at the final hurdle. The cat was so obstinate it wouldn't even help itself. He watched his mother rampaging towards him like a runaway train in a waterlogged nightdress. By rights, he should have been terrified, but he felt strangely calm. It dawned on him that he simply wasn't scared of her any more. After everything he'd been through, he knew that now, for the first time, he had the strength to stand up to her.

Koalas are pretty benign creatures. They hang about in eucalyptus trees, munching on leaves, sleeping, not really bothering anyone. But koalas can be extremely dangerous when they are sitting on the side of a hill in a raging storm. Lumpy and grey, they are particularly hard to see. Phillipa Slipper certainly didn't see this koala. She tripped over it, sending herself flying through the air like a human cannonball.

'Look out!' screamed Mrs Mandiddee.

Billy ducked as his mother soared over him. Her wild, matted hair lashed against his shoulders and her nightdress skimmed the top of his head. She clawed the air, arms flailing, spatula flapping. Her free hand grabbed beneath her, catching hold of

Jumblecat's tail. The astonished animal was plucked up and away with Phillipa Slipper and they flew, cartwheeling in a tangle of limbs. Both cat and mother tumbled and bumped, over hillocks through brambles, getting faster and faster, turning over and over, all the way down Tumbledown Hill and into the darkness of the night.

The storm blew out. A pale, silver moon muscled its way through the clouds, casting ghostly shadows across Tumbledown Hill. The rain dwindled, then stopped altogether. Billy, Mrs Mandiddee and a bruised Christopher Slipper zigzagged their way down the hillside. Every now and again, they called out, 'Jumblecat?' but he was nowhere to be seen. Nobody called out for Phillipa Slipper.

And then, from the shadows, a cat crossed their path. It was ginger, with patches on each of its paws, as if it had walked through a puddle of white paint. It strolled up to Billy and rubbed against his leg.

'Jumblecat? Is that you?' asked Billy softly. He got down on his knees and looked into the cat's green eyes. The cat nuzzled Billy's cheek, then rolled over, inviting Billy to tickle his tummy.

'Can you talk?' asked Mrs Mandiddee. The cat didn't reply, nor did it ask for a biscuit or complain about the wet grass. It just closed its eyes and purred deeply. It was a cat like any other cat.

'Come home with us,' said Billy. 'You can stay with Mrs Mandiddee, can't he, Mrs M?'

'Of course he can. He can stay for as long as he likes. I'll even change the wallpaper in the spare room.'

'I'll visit you every day. I can show you my Collectabillya and . . .'

Billy stopped talking. He realised that Jumblecat didn't understand. He was just a cat, after all.

Jumblecat rolled back onto his feet and sauntered off, sniffing at the wet grass as he went.

And what of Phillipa Slipper?

They found a spatula lying in the grass next to a large bramble patch full of ripe, juicy blackberries. Billy peered in. It was too dark to see.

'Is she in there?' asked Mrs Mandiddee, sounding none too concerned.

'I don't know. I can see something. It might be a rabbit,' suggested Billy

Christopher Slipper stepped forward. 'Phillipa? Can you hear me?'

The brambles shook.

'Are you all right?'

The brambles shook again, more vigorously this time.

Billy pushed his face deeper into the brambles. Slowly, his eyes adjusted to the prickly gloom. He saw a leg sticking up – she'd probably landed head first – and an arm and her head . . . but her head was way too close to her leg. It wasn't possible. It wasn't natural. He leapt back in shock.

'What's wrong?' asked Christopher Slipper.

'It's . . . er . . .' The words wouldn't come.

Christopher Slipper and Mrs Mandiddee took a look for themselves.

'Well I never!' exclaimed Mrs Mandiddee. She sounded quite tickled.

Christopher Slipper turned and faced Billy. His mouth hung open. 'She's . . .'

She looked just like Dobbie, Mindy's doll, with arms, legs and head all jumbled up in the wrong places.

We know by now that Billy's not a bad boy. Mischievous maybe, and something of a daydreamer, but not bad. Certainly not the kind of boy to leave his jumbled-up mother in a bramble patch. Surely he'd disentangle her from the bramble bush and take her back to the top of Tumbledown Hill?

Of course he would.

And, just as surely, he'd give her a gentle push down the hill and she'd be good as new. Good old Phillipa Slipper.

Of course he would.

Well, wouldn't you?

Acknowledgements

Enormous thanks to everyone who has helped and encouraged me along the way:

Dad, Sue, Bob, Shorts and my brilllllliant sister, Melissa (who in no way whatsoever bears any resemblance to Mindy), thank you all for your support and honest criticism from the outset;

To Emma Matthewson and all the fantastic team at Hot Key, as well as Kate Hindley for her superb illustrations;

To my agent, Jo Williamson, for getting the *Jumblecat* (fur)ball rolling in the first place;

To Mum, for providing my writing haven and the best gravy;

To Simon, for his unwavering belief, generosity and friendship;

And to Kasia, Otis and Matylda, my love forever.

About the Author

Ever since reading 'sodium monofluorophosphate' on the side of a toothpaste tube, Archie Kimpton has enjoyed putting words together and seeing what comes out. He graduated from Manchester University in 1991 and has spent the last twenty years in preparation for this moment of authordom – flogging salami, script writing, book binding and care working in the interim. *Jumblecat* is his first novel. He lives in south London with his wife, kids and Doonican, the diabetic cat and sometime-inspiration for his animal-cruelty-based stories. Follow Archie at www.archiekimpton.wordpress.com or on Twitter: @ArchieKimpton.

About the Illustrator

Kate Hindley lives and works in Birmingham (near the chocolate factory). She studied illustration at Falmouth College of Art, and went on to work as a children's print designer at a studio in Northampton, while working on children's books and greetings cards. She has exhibited with her good chums Girls Who Draw and Inkygoodness across the UK, and had a jolly good time painting up a totem pole for the Pictoplasma Character Walk exhibition in 2011. Kate's first picture book, *The Great Snorkle Hunt*, written by Claire Freedman, was published by Simon & Schuster in August 2013 and was longlisted for the 2013 Kate Greenaway Medal. Follow Kate at www.katehindley.com or on Twitter: @hindleyillos.

HOT KEY BOOKS

Thank you for choosing a Hot Key book.

If you want to know more about our authors and what we publish, you can find us online.

You can start at our website

www.hotkeybooks.com

And you can also find us on:

We hope to see you soon!